Harbor Nights

Rick Polad

**CALUMET
EDITIONS**

Chanhassen, Minnesota

FIRST EDITION MAY 2014

This is a work of fiction. Names, characters, places and incidents either are
the product of the author's imagination or are used fictitiously.

ISBN – 9781939548115

10 9 8 7 6 5 4 3 2 1

Cover art and book design by Gary Lindberg

Follow the author at:
www.rickpolad.com
www.facebook.com/spencermanningmysteries
@rickpolad

To Carol

"If I had a flower for every time I thought of you...
I could walk through my garden forever."
— Alfred Tennyson

Other Spencer Manning Mysteries

About the Author

Rick Polad teaches Earth Science, plays jazz trumpet, and volunteers with the Coast Guard on Lake Michigan. For over a decade, Rick has given editorial assistance to award-winning photographer Bruce Roberts and historian/author Cheryl Shelton-Roberts on several of their maritime-themed publications including *North Carolina Lighthouses: Stories of History and Hope,* and the third edition of *American Lighthouses: A Comprehensive Guide to Exploring Our National Coastal Treasures.* Rick also edited the English version of *Living With Nuclei,* the memoirs of Japanese physicist, Motoharu Kimura.

Acknowledgements

This book would not exist without the help and support of several special people. To my first readers and friends, Mike Polad, Carol Deleskiewicz, Gary Lindberg, Katie Tomlinson, Jonathan Roth, Tom Tallman, and Ellen Tullar Purviance, thanks for your edits and input. Any remaining errors are the property of the author. Thanks also to Jon Jarosh, Director of Communications and Public Relations, Door County Visitors Bureau. And, as before, to all my friends and readers who have asked for more Spencer, my undying thanks.

HARBOR NIGHTS

Chapter 1

Two boats motored into the channel between the peninsula and Plum Island. It was three a.m. They weren't showing any lights. One boat had a tarp covering something on the aft deck. They stopped midway between the two pieces of land and two men tied the boats together side-by-side. One man stepped over the gunwale onto the boat with the tarp. The other man pulled the tarp back and grabbed hold of two arms. The other grabbed the legs. They lifted a body onto the gunwale and rolled it into the water.

The first man climbed back onto his boat, untied the lines, and held onto the second boat with a boat hook.

"Okay, sink it," said the first man.

The second man took an axe and chopped a hole in the bottom of the wooden hull. He left the engine running in neutral. As the water started to flow in through the hole, the second man climbed onto the first boat and they slowly motored away. When they were four miles offshore in Lake Michigan, they turned on their running lights. Just two fishermen out early.

Chapter 2

I hate it when the phone rings in the middle of the night. Of course, middle is relative. It was eleven o'clock Friday morning, but I didn't get to sleep until seven.

I had been out with a friend comparing our lives and the success of the plans we had made in the sixties. Our lives didn't look anything like those plans we had made ten years ago while suffering through high school algebra.

I considered letting the machine get the call, but that would have meant five more rings and, as long as I had to listen to the ringing, I decided to answer. A groggy hello was the best I could manage.

"Spencer, it's Aunt Rose. Why do you sound like you're still asleep?"

I tried to come up with something witty, but given that it was the middle of my night, I came up short.

"Hello, Aunt Rose. Long story. There was this girl with a cowbell. She could…"

"Spencer! I don't care about the girl with the cowbell. Kathleen's been arrested."

I tried hard to pay attention but didn't totally succeed. "Kathleen?"

"Yes, Kathleen, you silly lout. The girl you almost married."

"Oh, that Kathleen. Well, technically…"

"Spencer!"

I sat up in bed and switched the phone to my right ear. "Arrested? Arrested for what?"

"I'm not exactly sure. I just got a panicked call from her from the jail. Something to do with stolen art. She asked me to call you and Rusty."

Wondering if I was dreaming, I said, "Rusty? Why would she have you call her uncle Rusty?"

In an exasperated voice, Rose replied, "I have no idea."

"Stolen art? Whose art?"

"I don't know that either. But seeing as how I have a detective in the family, I thought you could find out. They're taking her to Chicago."

Things didn't usually make sense in the middle of the night, and this was no different. "Why would Ephraim police take her to Chicago?"

"She wasn't arrested by Ephraim police—she was arrested by Chicago police."

"Why?"

"Stop asking why. That's why I called you—to find out why. Now get out of bed and do whatever it is you do to get to the bottom of things." Her voice raised several decibels. "The morning is almost gone for goodness sake!"

My eyelids closed and wanted to stay closed. Another exasperated *Spencer!* opened them. I asked for the number of the Ephraim police station. She gave it to me and I jotted it down.

"I'll see what I can find out."

"Good!" She hung up.

I held the phone out in front of me and listened to the dial tone. What happened to *goodbye*?

Kathleen and I were at one time thinking about getting married but never got to the final act, thankfully. Things would be going along just fine and then something would snap. She made a living as an artist, mostly painting harbor scenes, but I never quite understood how. Her father was the painter in the family and Kathleen hadn't exactly inherited his talent. He had a gallery in Door County, Wisconsin, which had provided a fine life for all concerned. That included Kathleen, two brothers, and their mother.

I met Kathleen the first summer my family started vacationing in Door County. I was twelve. When we grew older, our relationship grew into more than kids playing together. When we hit high school, we started to date, but it wasn't really any different from the time we had been spending together for years. Although we both dated others, the relationship became more serious in college. Aunt Rose liked Kathleen and told me I could do worse. To me, that wasn't a rousing endorsement.

Mom and Dad and I spent a month every summer at Aunt Rose's inn in Ephraim. The inn was a block from the gallery. Kathleen and I had a long-distance relationship through college that mostly consisted of a lot of fun in Door County for a month every summer. We would sail out to one of the is-lands where she showed me small limestone caves. She would bring her paints and I would bring detective novels. Mickey Spillane, Raymond Chandler, or Dashiell Hammett went wherever I did. I admit I was prejudiced, but Mike Hammer, Philip Marlowe, and Sam Spade were far better entertainment than Kathleen's paintings. She was built for fun summers, and I was smart enough to know a steady diet of Kathleen wouldn't be healthy. There were great times, but there were also crazy times.

Her father had showings in a gallery in Chicago several times a year, which gave Kathleen a reason to come to Chicago. He died a year ago, and the gallery had invited Kathleen to continue the showings. I never understood why—her paintings weren't that good. A year ago, a call from a client had rescued me from attending one of her shows. A few weeks ago, Aunt Rose had informed me that Kathleen would be having another show and would call me. I had started to make a list of excuses.

I called Stosh.

Chapter 3

Lt. Stanley Powolski answered in his usual *why are you bothering me on my private line* voice filled with all the charm of a billy goat.

"Morning, Stosh. Beautiful day to be alive."

"That depends on why you're calling. You canceling?"

Stosh and I had played gin and relaxed in front of the TV almost every Saturday afternoon for years.

"That depends. For the moment I'm looking for information. I just got a call from Aunt Rose. She says Kathleen Johnson has been arrested by Chicago police up in Door. Something to do with stolen art. You know anything about it?"

He sighed. "I do. An art dealer on Clark Street called on Wednesday. He said Kathleen stole a painting from his gallery."

"What gallery? The one where she shows her paintings?"

"If that's Simmons, then yes."

That did nothing to help my confusion. "I was hoping to get something from you to clear this up, but you're not helping."

He *humphed*. "Sorry. I am here to serve you. What's the problem?"

"What painting and why did they wait till this morning to arrest her?"

"Well, evidently she had shipped her paintings to the gallery for a showing and there was some confusion about them. They called us, then said there was nothing missing, and then called back and said there was."

"Pardon?"

"One of the employees saw Kathleen walk out with a painting on Wednesday. It still had the packing material around the frame. So they called and said a painting had been stolen. We sent an officer over there. When he got there, they told him they must have made a mistake because all the paintings were there."

"Did they explain that?"

"Yup. They called when the employee saw her walking out with a painting. While they were waiting for the officer, they counted her paintings, which were still in a crate that had been sent down from Door County. According to the order and the shipping list, there were supposed to be thirteen paintings."

"How many were there?"

"Thirteen. They apologized. The officer left. The next day, Thursday, we get another call making the same complaint—there's a missing painting."

"Was alcohol involved?"

"I don't need your smart-assed comments. They unpacked the crate on Thursday to put the paintings on display and there were only twelve. So they called back and filed a complaint."

"That doesn't make any sense. You sure about the alcohol?"

"Yes. And no, it doesn't."

"Did someone ask how the painting disappeared after Kathleen had left?"

"Yup. They assumed they had miscounted the first time."

"What was missing?"

"Something called *Harbor Nights*."

"Okay, so there's all this confusion. Bottom line is, they are her paintings. She sent them for the purpose of selling them. Why would she take one? And if she did, why would it be theft?"

"Evidently *Harbor Nights* was already sold. I figured we'd find out when we picked her up."

"Who arrested her?"

"Lonnigan and Steele. They questioned her. She said she did take a painting, but it was something called *Blue and Green*, which she said was hers. They asked her to produce it and she said she wouldn't."

"Strange. But sounds like Kathleen."

"And since the owner of the gallery swore out a complaint, they're bringing her back."

I glanced at the clock. They'd be back midafternoon. "Have Rosie call me when they get back."

"What happened to *please*?"

"Please."

He hung up. He and Aunt Rose could use a phone etiquette course.

I had known Rosie Lonnigan since high school. Our first topic of conversation was that she had the same name as my aunt. We had become great friends and attended the police academy together.

I like things to make sense and nothing about this did. But all the time I'd spent with Kathleen had taught me that very little of what she did made any sense. I had five hours to catch up on some sleep—after a few phone calls.

***

called the Ephraim police station. Chief Iverson answered.

"Good morning, Chief Iverson. My name is Spencer Manning. I'm calling to get some information about Kathleen Johnson who I understand was arrested this morning."

"And you are?"

"I'm a private detective in Chicago and a friend of Miss Johnson."

"Private detective, huh." He didn't sound too thrilled. "All I can tell you is we assisted with the arrest request from Chicago."

"Is she still there?"

"Nope. Left with two detectives about a half hour ago."

"Do you know anything about why she was arrested?"

"Yup."

I sighed. "And?"

"Do you remember the first thing I told you about all I can tell you?"

"I do. Thanks for your help."

I guess I couldn't blame him, but less sarcasm would have been nice. I was glad the case was in Chicago where I was used to a friendly conversation—most of the time.

***

My next call was to Ben, my favorite attorney. His hello was more cheerful.

"Morning, Ben. How are you enjoying leave?" Ben had told the State's Attorney's Office he was taking a year off from his public defender duties to re-evaluate his life.

"Pretty well, Spencer. Lots of golf and fishing."

"Any progress with the job problem?" After a sad ending to his last case and a girlfriend who walked out because she thought he shouldn't be defending criminals, Ben had taken some time off to think about what he wanted to do with his law degree.

"No. I know ignoring it isn't going to solve the problem, but thinking about it gets in the way of my golf swing. What's up?"

I laughed. "Kathleen has been arrested in Ephraim by Chicago police. They're bringing her back here."

"Arrested? What for?"

"Good question. It's a little strange. Theft of art."

"Okay, what's strange about that?"

"Well, it was her art. She had a showing at Simmons on Clark. Evidently she took one of the pieces back home to Door."

"Okay. Still don't see the problem."

"I don't know much, but evidently there was some confusion with the paintings. They kept changing their minds."

"About what?"

"About whether or not something was stolen, first of all. Then, she does admit to taking a painting, but she says it was a different painting than the one they say she took."

"Sounds like fun. And what do you want from me?"

"They'll be back here mid-afternoon. Please go to the bond hearing. I'll post bond."

"And after that?"

"Bring her back to my place and I'll find out what's going on."

"Okay. You going to be at home?"

"Yup. Late night. Gonna try and get a few more hours of sleep." I'd tell him later about the girl with the cow bell.

"Okay, I'll call when I find out times."

"Thanks, Ben. Much appreciated." I paused. I had just thought of something. "But don't be surprised if she doesn't make it to Chicago."

"What the hell does that mean?"

With a little smile Ben couldn't see, I said, "That means I just remembered something. Maybe nothing. Let me know."

"Sure, always fun playing games with you, Spencer. See ya."

"Yup."

My smile got bigger as I flopped back onto the bed. I had a guess as to why Kathleen had Aunt Rose call Rusty. Kathleen was one scrappy girl. I loved that about her—too bad the rest didn't work out.

Chapter 4

Sleep only lasted an hour until the phone rang again. It was Stosh.

"Spencer, Kathleen escaped."

My smile was back. My guess was right. "Hmmm, interesting."

"Hmmm, interesting. That helps a lot. You know something I don't?"

"From my humble abode in Chicago?" I asked innocently.

"Yeah, from your humble abode in Chicago."

"Next time you hear from Rosie, have her call me."

Stosh *humphed*. It was his trademark. "Sure, she's got nothing better to do, like looking for an escaped prisoner." He hung up.

I called Ben and filled him in. He had the afternoon off.

***

After all the interruptions I was wide awake, so I made some bacon and eggs and ate out on the deck. White, fluffy clouds and a slight breeze promised a nice day.

I had just finished the last piece of bacon when the phone rang.

"Morning, Spencer."

"Hey, Rosie. Bad day?"

"A whole week of bad days. What do you know about this?"

"Whoa, Detective. I just found out she was arrested a couple hours ago."

"And since then you have what?"

"A few questions."

She sighed. "If they're going to improve my day, ask."

She sounded discouraged, as well she should.

"Did she get you to stop along the way?"

"Yeah, said she had to pee."

"And would that have been at Gruber's Garage? Rundown gas station just over the canal before Sturgeon Bay? One pump out in front and junker cars scattered on the sides? And was there a green, battered, old pickup on the side of the garage by the bathroom?" That pickup hadn't moved in twenty years.

Silence. "Yes. And how do you know all this?"

"Didn't—lucky guess."

"Uh huh. Sure. Do I get an explanation or do I have you picked up as an accomplice?"

"For making a lucky guess?"

"No, for having information about a crime."

"I'm in Chicago, Rosie. All I know is she escaped."

"Sure, and all the rest? You just described the crime scene."

"I'm a detective—a good one. I take clues and make good guesses."

"Those aren't good guesses, Spencer—they're perfect guesses. And you know something I don't. She was your girlfriend. Did she call you?"

"She did not. Those were really just guesses, Rosie."

"This is serious, Spencer. Do you know where she is?"

"I do not. But if I hear anything, I'll call Stosh."

Her big exhale was loud and filled with exasperation. "Sure you will. Thanks for nuthin'. I'll find her myself."

"Good luck with that, Rosie."

I think she had hung up before hearing my good wishes. There was a click in there somewhere.

I knew I wouldn't hear from Kathleen. She had already sent her message by telling Aunt Rose to call me. She knew I would start looking into it. She also knew of my relationship with the police, and that if she did call I would have to tell someone. So I knew I wouldn't hear from her unless she was in big trouble

It didn't surprise me that Kathleen had escaped. That was one of the things I had loved about her. She was smart and very cunning. Rosie never had a chance. Most people call a lawyer with their one phone call. Kathleen had called my Aunt Rose and asked her to call the two people she needed help from—me and Rusty. Rusty, one of her uncles, is the nickname for Gus Gruber, the owner of the gas station where Rosie had stopped because Kathleen had to pee. Kathleen had escaped through the window of his gas station many times in high school, whenever she had a date she wasn't happy with. She would just disappear, leaving a hopeful teenage male wondering why he was suddenly alone. One memorable, hot Saturday night one of those hopeful males was me.

I felt badly for Rosie. She wouldn't find Kathleen. You couldn't walk fifty feet in Door County without bumping into one of her relatives, and they would all do whatever was needed to help her.

Chapter 5

After deciding I wasn't going to get any more sleep, I made two phone calls. One was to Aunt Rose to tell her I'd be there by dinner time. I asked if the cottage on Moonlight Bay north of Bailey's Harbor was being used. It wasn't. I also asked her to see if Maxine was free for dinner. A year ago, when I got Maxine the job with Aunt Rose, I had promised her a fish boil.

The other was to Kathleen's brother, Adam Johnson. He said he'd make himself available between five and six.

***

To save time, I took Highway 43 to Green Bay instead of the scenic route along the lake through Algoma, and crossed the bridge into upper Door County a little after four.

Adam was the manager at the Alpine Golf Resort just south of Egg Harbor. It was on the way to Aunt Rose's Harbor Lantern Inn in Ephraim. I parked, got out of the car, and scanned the course that had gotten the best of me more times than I could remember. Part of it was at road level and part up on a bluff. The eighth hole tee box was on the upper level. The green was on the lower. I always felt like I was hitting my ball off the edge of the world. You sent your clubs down on a cog tram. I passed the entrance to the clubhouse and turned right onto the road that led up to the top of the bluff where outcrops of tilted limestone disappeared into a farm field. During my summers in high school, Kathleen and I had found several small limestone caves.

I pulled off the road, got out, and looked out over the bay. The view out over the water to the north was spectacular and brought back wonderful memories of time spent with Kathleen sitting in the grass at this very spot. The tourists didn't come up here, so we were always alone with a view of the bay over the tops of the trees.

Adam was waiting in his office. The tired, worried look on his face told me the answer to my first question.

"Hello, Spencer. Been a while."

"It has, Adam. I'd like to say it's nice to see you but..."

"Yeah." He took a deep breath and let out a long sigh.

"I assume you haven't heard from her."

He shook his head. "No, I'm really worried. This doesn't make any sense. I know she behaves oddly at times, but this isn't like her. She'd get word to me somehow."

"She's also very smart and wily. She got away from two pretty good cops. Maybe she's just being careful."

"Do you think she's in danger?"

"I don't think so. If she was, I would've heard from her." I sat in a stuffed chair to the side of his desk. "This makes no sense to me either. Would you mind answering some questions?"

"Be my guest."

"Let's start with why would she be arrested for taking one of her own paintings?"

"There seems to be some confusion. The gallery in Chicago, Simmons, works with Kathleen and a frame shop up here called Framed. They do all of Kathleen's framing. They did Dad's also. Simmons sends Framed a list of the paintings they want to display. Somebody from Framed picks up the paintings on the list, they frame them, and then transport them to the gallery in Chicago."

That seemed strange to me. "Why doesn't Simmons deal directly with Kathleen?"

"That's easy. That's how they did it with Dad. Why they didn't deal directly with Dad I don't know. The kid..."

He was interrupted by a knock on the door frame.

"Unless you have something else, I'll be leaving, Mr. Johnson," said Adam's secretary.

"We're good Becky. If you can post the tournament list in the morning, that would be great. And there's the membership newsletter that needs to be sent to the printer. Sorry all this is falling at the same time. Have a good night."

She said goodbye and nodded to me.

Adam turned back to me and continued.

"The kid from Framed was supposed to come Saturday, but the owner, Gunderson, called and asked if he could come Sunday. Kathleen had to be in Milwaukee and her helper, Inga, couldn't make it, so I volunteered to open the door and let the kid in."

I wasn't sure why all that mattered. "Is that the normal procedure?"

"Yes, except for the day change."

"So, still wondering why she'd be arrested."

He shook his head. "I'm just guessing here, but I think the kid took a painting that wasn't supposed to go."

I waited.

"Kathleen has a favorite painting. She calls it *Blue and Green*. She has been offered three thousand dollars for it, but it isn't for sale."

"Why not?"

Adam shrugged. He looked exhausted. "I don't want to get into my crazy sister. You already know something about that."

I smiled. That was part of what I liked about Kathleen. She was unpredictable and a lot of fun. But it was also part of what I didn't like.

"She just won't sell it. She says it's her best work and it inspires her. I asked how much it would take for her to sell it and she just said it wasn't for sale."

"So?"

"So, I got a call from her when she got back on Tuesday. She wanted to know if I knew anything about *Blue and Green* being missing. I told her I didn't know it was. She was furious. We decided the kid from Framed took it by mistake.

"You said the kid had a list. How could he take the wrong painting?"

"Well, here's the confusion. There was a painting on the list called *Green and Blue*. It evidently was already sold along with several others. The kid could just have mixed up the names."

I tried to recreate the scene in Kathleen's shop. "So *Green and Blue* was left behind?"

Adam took a deep breath. "Well, that's the weird thing. It was gone, also."

"So what happened?"

"Kathleen called Gunderson. The paintings had already been driven down to Chicago by the kid. I told Kathleen to call the Chicago gallery in the morning and ask if *Blue and Green* was there."

"And what was their answer?"

"They didn't get the chance to answer. She was furious and said she'd drive down there herself."

"Not surprised by that," I said knowingly.

"No. She didn't trust any of them. The gallery had been trying to buy it, and she didn't put it past them to steal it if she wouldn't sell it."

I smiled. "Don't mess with Kathleen."

Adam agreed. "Yeah, she's a feisty handful."

"So, I'm assuming she got it."

"So am I."

"You don't know for sure?"

"No. I didn't hear from her. I didn't know anything was wrong until I got the call from you."

"And you still haven't heard from her?"

He shook his head again and looked very worried.

"Strange. But I don't think there's anything to worry about."

"Yeah, but until I get word of where she is, I'm going to worry. Where is she?"

"Good question. Another is why did she escape in the first place? Why not just go and clear up the confusion?"

Adam shifted in his chair. "Well, back to being unpredictable. She was pretty highly principled. She cared a lot more about what was right than she did about money. If she thought someone was trying to steal the painting, I have no idea what she would do."

"I agree, Adam. And the stories are conflicting. She says she took *Blue and Green* but one of the employees at Simmons saw her walking out with a painting under her arm. He says it was *Harbor Nights*, not *Blue and Green*."

Adam nodded. "And that raises another question. She went down there on Wednesday, but wasn't arrested until Friday."

"That one *I* can answer," I said. "When the manager of Simmons was told she had taken a painting, he checked the paintings to see which one was missing."

"And?"

"And none were. They were all there."

"All thirteen?"

"All thirteen."

Adam looked confused. "So..."

"Yup. So why was she arrested if none were missing? Well, that was Wednesday. When they were staging the paintings for display on Thursday, there were only twelve."

I got a strange look from Adam.

"My contact told me the manager, a Mr. Bloom, assumed the employee he asked to check on Wednesday miscounted somehow, and there were really only twelve on Wednesday. So Thursday, he calls the cops again."

Adam looked thoughtful. "Which one was missing?"

"*Harbor Nights*."

His eyes widened. "Why would she take *Harbor Nights*? She was trying to sell it."

I tried to make sense of this. "I have no idea, but it's missing and the employee says he saw her walking out with it. Maybe she was confused somehow."

He shook his head. "I doubt it. The kid might have been confused by the names, but she knows which is which. She painted the damned things. She went down to get *Blue and Green*. She wouldn't walk out with *Harbor Nights*. So where is *Blue and Green*?"

"Maybe *Blue and Green* is back in her studio."

"I thought of that," said Adam. "I checked the studio, her house, and her gallery in Ephraim. Not there. So we have a missing painting."

"Or maybe there's something we don't know—a missing piece to the puzzle that would explain all this. Maybe she *did* have a reason for taking *Harbor Nights*. But whatever happened, we have two missing paintings and a missing Kathleen."

"I'm just worried about Kathleen," said Adam. "I don't care about the paintings."

"Me too." I shifted in the chair and crossed my legs. "I'm guessing it's too soon to worry. She escaped, so she's probably holed up somewhere."

His forehead crinkled. "Why would she need to hole up?"

"Don't know. Any idea where that might be?"

"No. I've already made some calls. Could be anywhere. She has lots of friends and relatives who wouldn't ask questions. Any suggestions, Spencer?"

"Well, if you want answers you need to ask questions, and there are several people I have questions for, starting with Mr. Bloom down at Simmons."

Adam nodded. "Let me know if I can help."

"Will do. Actually, I'd like to get into her gallery and studio tomorrow if you're available."

"I can do better than that." He reached into his pocket and took two keys off of a ring. "The silver one is to the studio. Let me know if you find anything."

"Thanks, Adam. I'll be in touch."

He nodded again. I left his office, backed the Mustang out of the spot, turned right on Highway 42, and headed north to Ephraim.

Every case is a puzzle. And in every puzzle there's someone who knows where the pieces go. I just had to find that someone. And the sooner the better.

Chapter 6

I drove past Peninsula State Park and looked over the waters of Eagle Harbor out into Green Bay. Almost to the end of the curve around the bottom of the harbor, I pulled up the hill that led to Aunt Rose's Harbor Lantern Inn and felt like I was home.

I parked next to a family unloading their station wagon and walked up to the front porch where I found a new resident—a black cat—lounging on one of the wicker chairs. We stared at each other as I walked slowly across the porch. I stopped at the screen door as I reached for the handle and watched as the cat's eyes slowly closed.

Aunt Rose and Maxine were behind the front desk arranging the index cards Aunt Rose used to keep track of guests and their needs.

Maxine saw me first. "Spencer! What a nice surprise! Now I know who my mystery dinner date is."

I laughed and gave Maxine a hug. "And is this lovely lady your assistant?"

Aunt Rose put her arms around me and squeezed tight. "Spencer Manning, I don't know how you solve crimes with your mouth talking such nonsense."

I loved hugging Aunt Rose. She always smelled like pies. There was almost always a cherry pie in the oven.

"Who's the new resident on the porch?"

They both looked confused, but then Maxine remembered the cat.

"That's Amelie," she said lovingly.

"Come again?"

"Amelie." She spelled it. "Like homily, but with a silent h."

Rose explained. "We lost Torrey a month ago. I had said we should get another cat. He was such a part of this place for so many years. Then one day Maxine comes home with this scrawny thing she found out in the woods. We put out notices but no one claimed her. So we've fattened her up and taken her in. The kids love her."

I smiled. "She seems to have fallen into the routine very nicely."

"Yes," replied Rose, "the spirit of Torrey lives on." She glanced at her watch. "You two have reservations at Edgewater in a half hour and you want to get there in time for Maxine to see the boil, so I'll wrap up here and you two get going. Have fun."

The Edgewater Resort was just down the street and served two fish boil dinners on Friday nights. I got the key to the cottage from Rose and waited while Maxine changed. I was excited about being with her. It had been a while, but I had enjoyed the dinner we had in Chicago. She was a wonderful, down-to-earth girl who just needed a break in life.

***

Maxine filled me in on life at the inn as we sat on a wooden bench ten feet away from a boiling cauldron of water. When we got there, a man was lowering a wire basket of red potatoes and another filled with chunks of whitefish into the cauldron.

"Spencer, I can't begin to tell you how wonderful this all is. Aunt Rose is a sweetheart and this place is heaven. I don't know how to…"

I held up my hand. "You don't have to. The look on your face is thanks enough. I'm glad you like it. Looks like life up here is suiting you well."

"It really is, Spencer. But you'd have to about be dead for it not to. This is heaven on earth."

As a young couple sat down next to us, Maxine asked, "So, why are we sitting here watching a pot boil?"

I laughed. "You'll see."

A minute later, two men walked into the clearing. One was carrying a coffee can.

"What's in the can?" she asked.

"Kerosene."

She looked shocked. "Kerosene! For the fish?"

"Well, sort of." I smiled. "It's to burn off the fish oil."

"How…"

"Watch."

The man threw a cup of kerosene on the flames, which immediately roared. Within seconds, the pot boiled over and the men lifted the baskets out of the water.

Before Maxine could ask, I explained. "The increased heat causes the boil-over, which washes the oil out of the cauldron. Let's go eat." I took her hand and led her to the dining room.

After a wonderful dinner, we crossed the road and sat on one of the docks. A gentle breeze wafted in off the bay as we watched stars appear out of the twilight. The harbor was now dotted with red, green, and white running lights.

"I come down here a lot at night and watch the lights. It's mesmerizing. And I have no idea how all those boats avoid running into each other."

I laughed and tried to explain the navigation rules. "It's all about the lights. And you can tell which direction a boat is moving by which lights you see."

She thought for a minute. "Kinda like a stoplight. If you see red, you stop. If you see green, you go."

"Well, on paper. But you need common sense, too. The other guy isn't always going to stop. Always better to be alive than right."

We spent an hour with Maxine trying to tell me which way boats were moving and who should be waiting for whom. Toward the end of the hour she was getting most of them right.

***

I drove across the peninsula on Highway Q and turned down the road to Moonlight Bay. A half moon was just rising over the roof of the dark cottage. I dropped my bag in the kitchen, walked through the living room, and opened the drapes covering the sliding glass doors that looked out over the still waters of the bay. As I sat on a deck chair, an owl hooted from somewhere in the evergreens. And from farther off, the plaintive cry of a loon broke the silence.

I watched the moonlight shimmer on the water and wondered where Kathleen could be and why she had disappeared. Nothing made sense, but that was par for the course with her. In the morning I'd stop at the police station, the frame shop, and Kathleen's gallery and studio. For the moment, I just listened to the crickets and an occasional frog before falling asleep in the chair. I woke up at two a.m. and went to bed.

Chapter 7

I woke up at five Saturday morning and watched the sky turn from black to gray as the stars disappeared. Venus still shone brightly in the eastern sky about thirty degrees above the water.

I had planned to stop in at Framed when it opened at ten. I made some eggs and bacon, ate out on the deck, and looked forward to a sunny, hot Saturday. The weekend forecast was for clear skies and breezes off the bay, which would help keep the heat down.

At eight, I called the Ephraim police station. I recognized the voice that answered.

"Ephraim Police, Sergeant Gruber. How may I help you?"

"Hello, Paul. Spencer Manning."

"Spencer! I figured we'd be hearing from you. Long time no see."

"But always a pleasure." Paul was two years younger than me and had always wanted to be a policeman. We had spent a lot of time on the water during my high school summers. He was the grandson of Gus Gruber, better known as Rusty, and had often joined Kathleen and me on our summer adventures.

He laughed. "Maybe not so much this time, eh? Our Kathleen seems to have gotten the best of Chicago's finest."

"They never had a chance," I said cheerfully. "You going to be there a bit? I'd like to stop by."

"Sure. Chief's out on a call. I'll be here."

"Great. Be about a half hour."

I hung up and cleaned up breakfast. The rinsed dishes went into the dishwasher. I used so few dishes that I often washed them by hand and used the dishwasher for a dryer.

The Ephraim Police Department had doubled in size a year ago when they hired Paul. Before that there had just been the chief. Technically, they called Paul a constable. They were the only town in upper Door that had a police force, if you call two a force. The peninsula was patrolled mostly by the County Sheriff's office out of Sturgeon Bay, but crime was minimal and usually not serious, so there wasn't much need for the sheriff. There was only one road into the peninsula. Most people didn't even bother locking their doors.

***

Paul was sitting at his desk doing paperwork when I walked in. We shook hands, caught up a bit, and then I sat on the wooden chair at the side of his desk.

"You know anything about this craziness, Paul?"

He shook his head. "I'm just as confused as you. But then I never have been able to figure out that girl."

"You and me both. Were you here when she was brought in?"

"Well, sort of."

"Sort of?"

He folded his hands on top of the desk. "Is this off the record?"

"Shouldn't I be the one asking that? I'm not in charge of the record."

His eyes locked on mine and he looked like he was trying to make a decision.

"I was the one who took the call from Chicago. That was at seven a.m. I was told that two detectives were on their way to get Kathleen, and I was asked to pick her up for questioning."

"And you went out to get her?"

"Well, not exactly."

I spread my hands, palms up, and stared back at him. "So give me the exactly."

"Between you and me, right?"

"Don't see why not."

"There's that law thing."

"Unless you killed her, I don't see a problem."

Even though it was clear we were the only ones in the office, he looked around.

"I didn't kill her. But I didn't pick her up either. I called her and told her about the call from Chicago."

I'm sure my face showed surprise. "Not exactly standard procedure."

"Not exactly. Hence the problem."

I shook my head. "Don't see why. She did get picked up eventually. And you weren't the one who lost her. So what happened?"

"She said she would come in on her own but asked for a few hours. I said sure, but made it clear she had to be here by the time the Chicago detectives showed up or my ass was in a sling."

"And she obviously agreed."

"She did. And at a little after eleven she showed up."

"Did you ask why she wanted a few hours?"

"Yes. She wouldn't tell me."

"Not surprised. And what did you two do while you waited?"

He shrugged. "We just sat and chatted. I asked her what it was all about. She said she didn't know and swore she didn't steal anything."

"No. Of course not. Any idea where she is?"

He shook his head. "I checked the obvious places with the Chicago detectives, and then a couple not so obvious on my own. Nothing. I made a few calls. Either someone is lying or she's disappeared—and I don't rule out the first."

"No, me either. Pretty close bunch, these Johnsons. How about the Chicago detectives? Know where they are?"

"Not a clue." He straightened in his chair. "They've been working with the sheriff and chief."

I handed him my card. "Do me a favor and give me a call if you find anything. Use the pager number."

"Sure. But I don't think I'm in the loop. I get the feeling they don't trust me—me being related."

"Well, if you do."

"Sure, Spencer. What are you going to do?"

"Talk to a few people and see if I can make sense of this. Going to start with Framed over in Fish Creek. Who am I likely to find there this morning?"

"Edvard Gunderson, the owner. And he's got a kid who runs errands and helps with the framing."

"Yeah, that would be the kid who picked up the paintings. You know his name?"

He smiled mischievously and tilted back his chair. "Cletis Muddd."

My face must have shown my surprise. Paul laughed.

"Not from around here, I'm guessing."

"Hardly. He's from Tennessee."

"How do you know that?"

"Gunderson asked us to look into his past when the kid applied for the job a few months ago."

"That's a little strange. Do you always check backgrounds for normal jobs?"

"No. I thought it strange, too, so I asked him about it. I didn't get a good answer. He just said he had a reason to ask and would greatly appreciate it."

"You find anything?"

He shrugged. "Not much. Marijuana possession, a theft charge that was dropped."

I nodded. "Lotsa kids up here. Why would he hire someone with a background like that? Even if it was a minor offense."

"Seemed strange to me, too. No clue. And by the way, the last name is spelled with three Ds."

"You're kidding."

"Nope."

"Who the hell would do that?"

"No one. I checked on the parents and their name only has two. So my guess is someone screwed up on the birth certificate and the parents let it ride. Makes a nice conversation piece."

"Strange."

"And here's somethin' else. The kid lived in Chicago before he came up here."

"Hmmm. You have an address?"

"Yup." He waved at the stack of files on the counter. "If you want to spend hours trying to find the report, be my guest."

I nodded toward the counter. "Nice filing cabinet."

"We're a little short of help. You going to look for her?"

I stood. "Gonna try, but if she doesn't want to be found, she won't be. Thanks for your help, Paul."

He set his chair back down and we shook hands.

I hadn't learned much, but I had a few more bits of information that might fit somewhere in the puzzle. And it was nice seeing Paul.

Chapter 8

Mid-June was always pretty predictable in Door County. Mild temperatures and sunny days were a joy compared to the heat and humidity of July that brought some pretty severe storms. Saturday morning was gorgeous—72 degrees and a few puffy, white cumulus clouds drifting across the sky.

My next stop was Framed in Fish Creek. The shop was at the edge of town. An empty lot separated it from the Village Hall and the row of restaurants, art galleries, and various other stores that lined both sides of the street. It was a little before ten o'clock and the sidewalks were not yet crowded. I was able to get a parking spot on the street in front of a frozen yogurt stand across from Framed. By noon, the sidewalks would be crowded with tourists and open parking places would be rare.

The shop looked like an old cottage. Two large picture windows showed off dozens of frames. A *Closed* sign hung in the window to the right of the door. I sat on a bench across the street and waited. The opening time, ten o'clock, was stenciled on the door.

At ten minutes after ten, the lights came on and someone took down the *Closed* sign and unlocked the door. It was an older man, probably the owner, Mr. Gunderson. I waited a few more minutes and then strolled across the street.

When I opened the door, the man behind the counter turned and uttered a very prim and proper good morning.

"Good morning. Nice day." I tried to sound friendlier than him.

He smiled stiffly. Always smile at a customer, whether you mean it or not. "Yes, this is a beautiful time of year. I'll be right with you. My employee didn't show up this morning."

While he got the cash register ready I looked around the store. There were two main rooms—the one I was in, and a larger room through an open doorway. I could see several counters and frames in various stages of construction.

The man finally stepped around the counter and asked how he could help me. He looked to be about sixty, was about my height, a bit overweight, and balding.

"Well, I'm looking for some information."

"Of course. What are you looking to have framed?"

"Not that kind of information. I have some questions about one of your customers."

"And who would that be?"

"Kathleen Johnson."

He lost the smile and stepped back.

A customer came in.

He looked at me defiantly, probably hoping I would leave.

"I'll wait."

He turned and asked the woman how he could help. He wasn't happy that I had walked into his store. I considered myself a pretty nice guy, but I sometimes had that effect on people.

They chatted for a few minutes before she left without buying anything.

He walked back to the other side of the counter. Back there he was in charge.

"Kathleen Johnson?" he asked warily.

"Yes, are you Mr. Gunderson?"

He nodded. "And what questions do you have about Kathleen Johnson?"

I leaned against the counter. "She's missing and I'd like to find her."

"Are you with the police?"

"No. Private."

"Do you have ID?"

I showed him my Wisconsin license.

He looked at the license, then at me, then back at the license. "And who are you working for, Mr. Manning?"

"No one. She's a friend."

"I see." He sat on a stool. "And why do you think I can help?"

I knew he knew why I thought he could help, but he didn't know how much I knew.

"I understand you framed some of her paintings and shipped them to Chicago."

"My help framed them."

I waited but he offered nothing else.

"And I understand there was some confusion with the paintings."

"Confusion?" He looked surprised.

"Yes, something about her favorite painting being taken, and then two paintings disappearing from the gallery in Chicago."

"I did hear about that. Very worrisome. I understand the police are looking into it."

I nodded. "They are. But I have some questions."

He looked nervous. His lip quivered and he was rubbing his hands together. "Well, I really don't have much time. There is a lot to do to get ready for the day."

"I'll be quick and would really appreciate your help."

"Well, okay, as long as it is quick."

I flipped pages in a catalog on the counter and said, "I understand there were thirteen paintings taken for display and some were already sold. Correct?"

"Yes. That often happens. Someone pre-buys a painting and then the sold painting is used kind of like a pump primer. No one wants to be the first to make a purchase."

"Makes sense. But what I don't understand is why she was arrested for taking her own painting."

"Evidently you don't know the whole story. There was another missing painting. She may have taken that one."

"Just to be clear, we're talking about *Blue and Green* and *Harbor Nights*. Right?"

He sighed. "Yes."

I leaned on the counter. "And *Blue and Green* was her property, and should not have been shipped to Chicago. Do you know how that happened?"

"I did ask my hired boy about that. He says he was confused by the names. There also was a *Green and Blue*. He thinks he put both paintings in the crate when he loaded the paintings from her gallery. He's not the smartest kid. I wasn't happy about hiring him in the first place."

"So why did you?"

"Well, let's just say he had friends in Chicago who suggested strongly that I hire him. But he made mistakes and I warned him I might have to let him go if he kept making them."

I nodded. "Could be he mixed them up. But did *you* know that *Blue and Green* wasn't on the list?"

"I guess it wasn't. I had tried to buy that from her but she wouldn't sell."

I slid down a few feet closer to him. "So why did you frame it and send it to Chicago?"

He grabbed onto the edge of the counter and straightened. "I didn't. The boy does the framing. I just do the paperwork and make sure he makes the delivery."

"I see. So you never saw the paintings?"

"I saw them. But the boy handled them."

"That would be Cletis?"

He nodded.

"I'd like to talk to him. Do you know where I can find him?"

He frowned at me. "You *should* find him here. But as you can see, he *isn't* here—on my busiest day."

"When did you last see him?"

"He was at work yesterday. He left at five."

"Does he work every day?"

"No, just three days a week."

"Has Kathleen been in touch with you lately?"

"No. No, she hasn't."

I handed him my card and asked him to call if he heard anything, or if Cletis showed up. He said he would, but I had the feeling he was just saying it to get rid of me. I made him nervous, but I didn't know why. I had the feeling it was more than just confusion over the paintings.

I turned toward the frozen yogurt stand after I walked out. I glanced back through the window and saw Mr. Gunderson making a phone call. I had stirred a pot, but I had no idea what was in it.

Chapter 9

When I finished the yogurt, it was close to eleven and the sidewalks were crowded. I had two more stops I wanted to make—Kathleen's gallery and her studio. I took Highway 42 back to Ephraim. Her gallery, Color My World, was about a block up the street from the harbor. The small parking lot in front of the row of shops was full so I drove the few blocks back to the inn, parked, and walked back. I turned at Wilson's Ice Cream and went up the hill to the gallery.

Adam had told me the manager was Inga and that he would call and tell her I was a friend. She was busy with a customer so I browsed the paintings. I wasn't impressed with most of them. Good thing for Kathleen I wasn't an art critic.

I watched Inga talking with a male customer about a foot taller than her. She was a little blond, about five-foot-four with short, straight hair, rosy cheeks, and blue eyes. She wore a bright, flower-patterned dress that just covered her knees, and a white pullover cotton top. She was telling the man about Kathleen's style of painting. It sounded like she knew what she was talking about, but it made no sense to me. When the man left, I walked over and introduced myself.

She smiled. "Yes, Mr. Johnson told me you'd be stopping by. How can I help?"

"It you have a few minutes, I have some questions about the paintings."

"Sure. Would you like to sit?"

We sat on a padded bench in the middle of the gallery.

"I'm trying to understand what happened with the paintings. This green blue, blue green thing is confusing."

She took a deep breath. "I agree. I told her so when she named the second one, but she thought it would be cute."

"Which one was second?"

"Oh, *Green and Blue*. She had painted *Blue and Green* years ago. It was her favorite."

"I heard she refused to sell it—turned down thousands of dollars."

"That's true." She turned toward the door when a couple walked in and told them to ask if they had any questions. "It didn't make any sense to me, Spencer, but that was Kathleen."

"Was *Blue and Green* exceptional somehow?"

She bit her lip. "Between you and me, I didn't think so." She hesitated. "But she had some personal connection to it."

I sighed. "Yes, hard to figure her out sometimes. I'm wondering how *Blue and Green* got sent to Chicago. Mr. Gunderson said he asked Cletis, who said he was confused by the names."

"As I already said, I'm not surprised by the confusion. Cletis is a nice kid, but not the brightest."

"Was *Blue and Green* here?"

She shook her head. "No, she kept it at her studio—said it gave her inspiration."

"So how could the kid take a painting from the studio?"

"That didn't help with the confusion. Four of the paintings were already sold. They were here. The rest were at the studio. So we decided to bring the four from here over to the studio so they would all be together and Cletis wouldn't have to make two stops. I wish I had been there—I would have made sure he took the right ones. Adam didn't know."

"The paintings here are all framed. Were the nine at the studio also framed?"

"No, just the four. And those were actually re-framed before they were sent to Chicago."

I turned and straddled the bench. "Why?"

"Whoever bought them ordered custom frames from Mr. Gunderson."

"And had the people who bought them seen them here in the gallery?"

"Oh, no. They bought them from photos that Mr. Gunderson took."

"Isn't that strange?"

Inga shrugged. "Maybe. But he has connections in Chicago and has sold many of her paintings. Can't turn down business. Miss Johnson has sold more paintings down at the Simmons Gallery than she has sold here. So she follows Mr. Gunderson's directions."

"Seems like a strange setup."

She cocked her head and sighed with resignation. "Yes, but it pays the bills, and there was never any problem, so I just accepted it."

I nodded. "Do you know who the buyers are?"

"No. As far as we're concerned, the purchase is by Framed. The check comes from there, also."

"Did Kathleen come here often?"

"Three or four mornings a week. She'd have tea with me and chat with customers. She'd leave before noon. She liked to paint in the afternoon when the light was good."

The woman who had come in asked for help.

"I'll be right with you, ma'am. Will you excuse me, Spencer?"

"Just one more question. Was *Green and Blue* here or at the studio?"

"It was here."

"So it was one of the paintings to be re-framed?"

"Yes."

"And *Blue and Green* was at the studio?"

"Yes."

"Okay, thanks, Inga. You've been a big help." I gave her a card and repeated the instructions.

***

drove back to the cottage and called Stosh. He answered with his usual lack of enthusiasm.

"You must be behaving yourself. I haven't had any calls from Wisconsin."

"So far I don't know enough to piss off anybody."

"Try and keep it that way. Why am I blessed with this call?"

"Wondering where Rosie is. Have you heard from her?"

"She and Steele are on their way back."

"Not looking for Kathleen?"

"That's up to the sheriff. When he finds her we'll bring her back here."

"*When*? I'm betting on *if*."

"No one can hide forever."

"That's part of the problem, Stosh. There's no reason she should be hiding. It was her painting. And even if she took the one that was sold, she just needed to bring it back. We must be missing something."

"We are. Your girlfriend."

He could bait me with that girlfriend crap as much as he wanted. I wasn't biting—this time. "Have you found the other missing painting?"

"If you mean *Harbor Nights*, no. Which brings up a question." He paused. "Steele ain't an artist, but he tells me your girlfriend's paintings weren't very good. How do you think she got into a fancy gallery like Simmons?"

"I've wondered that myself. I wouldn't have bought one. She was nowhere near as talented as her dad."

"So, back to my question," he said, impatiently.

"No idea. Lots of things don't make any sense. Have you asked at Simmons?"

"That's on Rosie's agenda for Monday."

"Okay. Would you have her call me tonight? I'll be at the cottage."

"I'll pass on the request, but you're not real high on her list these days."

"Don't see why not—*I* didn't lose Kathleen."

"If she calls, I suggest you don't remind her of that."

"Right."

"When are you coming back?"

"Probably tomorrow. I have some questions for the people at Simmons."

"Sure you do. If you get back before the end of the Cubs game, stop by."

***

My next stop was Kathleen's studio, next to her house on Kangaroo Lake, and it was lunchtime. So I decided to stop for lunch at the Coyote Road-house on the west side of the lake. Best burgers in the county. And, as I remembered, Kathleen's favorite spot for lunch. She could walk from her house. I wondered if Paula was still the hostess.

Chapter 10

The Coyote Roadhouse was crowded. Most of the tourists never ventured to the interior of the peninsula. They stayed on Highway 42 along Green Bay where most of the shops and attractions were. The locals avoided the crowds and had their favorite restaurants off the beaten path. One of those was the Coyote Roadhouse. It had been there as long as I could remember.

I stood inside the front door and looked around. I hadn't been there in five years, but not much had changed—booths along the walls, tables on the floor, a small bandstand in the far corner, all decorated with a fishing and lighthouse motif. Paula was in the back by the bandstand wiping down a table. I leaned against the counter by the cash register and waited. When she saw me, her face lit up with a smile. She made her way between the tables and back to the register.

"Spencer Manning. What a surprise. I thought you forgot about your old friends."

"Not forgotten, Paula, just too darned busy. How the heck are ya?"

"Not too bad for an old broad." She still had the smile.

"Not that old, and not too bad for any broad, Paula."

"Still a charmer, eh?" And then she lost the smile and frowned. "I'm guessing you're not here to eat. Kathleen has kept us up on your career. Pretty exciting."

"Sometimes it is exciting. And yes, I'd like a few minutes of your time, but I *am* hungry and hoping you're still serving burgers."

She smiled again with bright lively eyes. "Of course! Why don't you take one of the booths by the window and by the time you're done eating I should be able to spare a few minutes."

"Great. Thanks."

Paula dropped off a Schlitz and fifteen minutes later a waitress I didn't recognize brought a mushroom cheddar burger and fries. I ate slowly and savored each juicy bite as I watched the crowd.

Paula appeared as I finished the last bite. The Coyote was a local favorite because of her. She ran it like the captain of a ship, but with a velvet touch rather than an iron fist. Her commanding presence kept everything running smoothly with a kind word and an encouraging smile. She relaxed as she slid into the booth opposite me.

"I'm assuming you're here about Kathleen. Gretchen is covering the door for me, but I'll have to go if there's a rush."

"No problem. What have you heard?"

She leaned toward me and spoke quietly. "News gets around pretty fast up here. I heard last night that she was arrested and cops from Chicago were taking her back to Chicago when she escaped. I don't know exactly what it's all about—something about stolen paintings."

I laughed and emptied the bottle of Schlitz. "That's some grapevine you've got. That's about it."

Her brow furrowed and she looked puzzled. "But *it* doesn't make sense. Weren't they her paintings?"

"Yup. And I'm just as confused as you. It *doesn't* make sense."

"Are you looking for her?"

"Poking my nose around, but she'll be pretty hard to find if she wanted to disappear. I'm also trying to follow the painting trail. It's pretty confusing. When was the last time you saw her?"

She sighed and squinted. "That would have been a week ago, Friday."

"How often does she come in?"

"Three or four times a week. And always on Wednesday for the meatloaf special. I was surprised when she didn't show."

I remembered the meatloaf—worth a trip. "Did she seem normal that Friday?"

"Yes, same old chitchat. I remember her saying that the light would be great with the clear sky."

"And you haven't heard anything from her?"

She shook her head with obvious concern.

Gretchen called her and I saw a line of customers at the counter.

"Gotta go, Spencer."

I gave her my card and told her to call the pager if she heard anything.

"Nice to see you, Spencer."

"You also, Paula. Take care."

She winked.

I paid and headed south on Kangaroo Lake Road. Kathleen's studio was only a half mile down the road, just past the faded-red barn where we used to hide from her cousins. She had little patience with most people, even as a kid, but for some reason she had put up with me.

Chapter 11

Kathleen's studio was just south of her ranch house and set on the back of the lot. I pulled the Mustang into the gravel drive and parked next to the house. Kangaroo Lake was a few hundred feet to the east. A wooden dock with a canoe tied to it jutted out from the bank. The lake was long and skinny. I could see across to the east side. A wooden deck with lawn chairs and a hammock was inviting me to spend a few hours. The warm sun and a light breeze would have made for a nice nap. Maybe I would head down there after checking out the studio. I had no idea what I was looking for, but I wanted a look around.

As I approached the front door, I hesitated. It was ajar. I looked in through the windows to make sure I wasn't surprising anyone. The only one surprised was me as I pushed the door open and walked into a mess. Paintings and supplies were scattered around, drawers were pulled out and dumped on the floor, and papers were strewn all over. Someone was obviously looking for something and I guessed they hadn't found it.

Not wanting to touch the phone, I drove back to Coyote and called the Ephraim police from Paula's office. I got a woman who said her name was Barb and said she would get ahold of Chief Iverson.

I hung up and called Adam. His secretary answered.

"Hello, I need to talk to Adam Johnson, please."

"I'm sorry, he's out on the course. We're in the middle of a tournament."

"I know. But I really need to talk with him. It's about his sister."

I explained who I was and she said she would send someone to get him.

I waited five minutes.

"Hello, Spencer. You've got something?" He still sounded worried.

"Well, yes. I stopped at the studio. Someone broke in and trashed the place."

Silence. "What the hell, Spencer? That makes no sense."

I took a deep breath. "Well, no and yes. Someone was looking for something."

"The paintings?"

I sat in Paula's desk chair. "I don't think so. This has to be about something else."

"What?" he asked in a shaky voice.

"No idea. But this might explain why Kathleen disappeared. The police were looking for her and then she discovered that someone had broken into her studio. She suddenly felt threatened and went someplace she'd feel safe. Any ideas?"

"That could be a number of places. There are a lot of people who would hide her."

"Yup. And that's good. I'm betting she's okay." I tried to sound reassuring, but after finding the mess I wasn't so sure.

"I hope you're right."

"Me too. When was the last time you were at the studio?"

"Friday, late afternoon, when I went to look for the painting."

I stood up and sat on the desk. "So this happened Friday night or early this morning."

"Yeah. Do you want me to come over? I'm pretty busy here."

"I don't think so. If the police want you, they'll call. But the door lock is broken. See if you can get someone to get that fixed."

"I'll get my secretary on it. Let me know if you find anything, Spencer."

"Will do, Adam."

I headed back to the studio. While I was waiting, I walked around the house and checked the doors and windows. There were no signs of forced entry. Ten minutes later Chief Iverson pulled into the drive.

***

Hello, Manning," he said with no emotion. "Trouble seems to follow you around."

"How so, Chief?"

"I seem to recall a little incident a year ago."

"Well, as *I* recall, the trouble got there before I did."

Without replying, he led the way to the studio.

"What a mess." He walked through the building. "Any idea what they were looking for?"

"Nope. But it wasn't a painting." Drawers had been pulled out and emptied. "Had to be small enough to fit in a drawer."

He glared at me and didn't respond. I knew I wasn't going to get any questions answered so I didn't ask any. But I was willing to bet the sheriff would take over and Iverson wouldn't be happy about that. Iverson was in a tough position, and I sort of felt sorry for him. But it didn't last long. He wasn't the kind of guy who engendered much sympathy, not that he was looking for any.

He walked back to the door. "Lock's broken."

"Adam is calling someone to come and fix it."

He didn't respond.

I turned toward the door. "If you don't need me, I'm heading back to Chicago." I was sure he didn't need me and would be glad to see me go.

With his back to me, he said, "Have a nice trip."

Keeping my response to myself, I walked to the car and drove back toward the cottage. On the way, I picked up a steak, a potato, and a six pack. I did plan on heading back to Chicago, but not until Monday morning. I was going to relax and wait for Rosie's call. I figured she still thought I knew more than I had told her and would still be upset, but I hoped she would want to chat.

While I'd been brightening the chief's day, the sky had grown overcast and the humidity had risen. As I drove through Bailey's Harbor, I heard a rumble of thunder. I made it back to the cottage before it started to rain and stood on the deck as big drops started to plop into the bay.

Chapter 12

sprawled on the couch and watched the storm roll out over Lake Michigan. When the rain stopped, I grilled the steak, added sour cream and butter to the potato, and poured a Schlitz. I ate on the deck and watched two canoes gliding across the bay. It had been a long day and I fell asleep in the deck chair wondering what Kathleen had gotten herself into.

The ringing phone woke me at ten fifteen.

"Hello, Spencer, hope it's not too late."

She sounded tired and defeated.

"No, it's fine, Rosie. You still mad at me?"

"Still! I teach a course in being mad at you. I have a waiting list." She was silent for five seconds. "But I'm more mad at me. I know you wouldn't help someone escape. She got the best of me. I feel like such a fool."

I took the phone to the couch and sat down. "You're not the first, Rosie. Don't blame yourself. And if it helps any, I don't think she did anything wrong."

"And what's that based on? One of your gut feelings?"

I sighed. "Well, yes, and no. I've known her for a long time. She's smart and she's pretty screwy, but I'd bet my life on her honesty."

"So, what's the *no* part?"

"There's more to this than just a missing painting."

"That sounds like a gut feeling."

I laughed. "I guess it is, but there's more to it. Two missing paintings and confusion about the names. And have you heard about her studio?"

"No, what about it?"

"Someone broke in and trashed it."

"Looking for something," she said. "Any idea what it was?"

"No. But drawers were emptied so it wasn't a painting."

"Interesting. But you said she's smart. Maybe she staged it all. Maybe this is all about Kathleen."

"Could be, but I'd bet not. And there's another missing person."

"Really? Who?"

"Cletis Muddd, with three Ds."

"The helper at the frame shop? Three Ds? What are you talking about?"

"His last name—M U D D D."

"You're kidding."

"Nope. Constable Gruber ran a background check before Muddd was hired. Figures it was a mistake by whoever filled out the birth certificate and the parents left it."

"Just when you think you've heard it all. But why do you think he's missing?"

"Missing is perhaps the wrong word. Disappeared may be better. I stopped by Framed this morning. The owner, Gunderson, wasn't happy. The kid didn't show up for work. He tried calling Muddd's apartment and got no answer."

"Doesn't mean he disappeared."

"No, but add it to the list of oddities."

"How long are you staying up there?"

"Coming back Monday morning."

"You're not going to stay and look for her?"

"No. I'll do some more poking around tomorrow and I have a few ideas."

"Are you worried about her?"

I took a deep breath. "I wasn't at first, but I am now that I saw the studio. But she has a lot of family and friends up here who would be more than willing to hide her. If she needs me, she'll call."

"And if she does call?"

Then I'll call you. There are some people I'd go to jail for, but she's not one of them."

She was quiet. I hoped she believed me, but I wasn't going to ask.

"What *are* you going to do, Spencer?"

"I want to check out the Chicago part of this puzzle. What do you know about the Simmons Gallery?"

"Not much. After some confusion, they reported a painting as stolen and the kid who works there said he saw Kathleen walking out with it."

I put my feet up on the coffee table. "That would be *Harbor Nights*?"

"Right."

"Did he actually see the painting she walked out with?"

"Well, I don't know. But that's the painting that's missing."

"So he may have just assumed that was the painting," I said.

"What else would it be?"

I explained the confusion with the names. "I don't see her having any reason for taking *Harbor Nights*. She was trying to sell it."

"But it *is* missing."

"Yeah, strange. Are you going back there?"

"Me! Really? I lost their suspect. That's the last place I want to be! When we find her, we'll get them for an ID."

"I hate to ask, but would you do me a favor?"

"Depends. What?"

"Run this Cletis Muddd. Paul said he moved to Door from Tennessee with a stop in Chicago. I'd like to know where."

"You think he's involved?"

"Theft and a missing suspect and the kid disappears. What do *you* think?"

"Yeah, weird. Let me know how Simmons goes."

I sat up and glanced out the picture window. An almost-full orange moon was rising out of the water, looking twice as big as it does up higher in the sky. "I'm going to stop there Monday morning. How 'bout lunch?"

"Well, if you don't mind company, sure."

"Company?"

"We have a new detective reporting Monday—Brenda Pitcher. I'm taking her to lunch."

"Fine with me. Does this mean Steele has a new partner?"

She laughed. "Usually, but I kinda like the guy. Don't know if I want to give him up."

"I thought he drove you nuts."

"He does, but he's growing on me. He can be frustrating, but just when I decide I've had it he does something extraordinary."

"Okay, your funeral. Where and when for lunch?"

"Molly's—noon."

"See you then, Rosie. Get some sleep."

"Night, Spencer."

I watched the man in the moon smiling down on the bay for a few minutes and then headed for bed. I had been up since five and was beat.

Chapter 13

Simmons was a typical storefront on Clark Street just south of Belmont. Lots of glass with paintings displayed in the windows. I got there at ten-thirty Monday morning and walked in. A bell over the door rang. There was no one in sight, but there were signs of activity. It looked like paintings were in the midst of being displayed in the main room off to the left. They were Kathleen's. I looked through a break in the middle of the wall into another room and saw a wall filled with clown pictures. I had always been leery of clowns.

Dad took us to the circus every year at the Masonic Temple. Mom loved the clowns. They were her favorite part. Mine was the acrobats, and the music. There was something about the clowns that bothered me. Mom just gave me a hug and laughed. One of my friends called me a scaredy-cat, but I wasn't scared—I just didn't trust them. What were they hiding?

I faced my nemesis and looked at the clown paintings. I was in the back corner when a man came into the main room without noticing me and started placing paintings on easels. He looked to be in his fifties, was nicely dressed in an immaculately tailored blue suit, and had beady eyes and too much forehead. I could have watched for a while and learned something about placing paintings, but I had better things to do. I walked up to a few feet behind him and cleared my throat. He jumped and turned around with a look of fear.

"Oh my. I'm sorry. You startled me. I didn't see you there."

I backed up a few feet. "Sorry, didn't mean to scare you. I got caught up in watching you work."

His eyes closed a bit, he sort of shivered, and then looked puzzled. "And you are?"

I held out a card. "Spencer Manning. I'm a friend of Kathleen Johnson."

It was quick, but he flinched. He recovered well.

"And you are here because…" he said slowly and carefully.

"Just trying to get some culture. Interesting clown exhibit."

He sighed. "That's not exactly my idea of culture. My assistant set that up—he likes clowns, and, more importantly, so does a wealthy benefactor. The only one I like is the sad one—some pretty strong emotions there. So, why are you really here?"

He hadn't bought my culture story. "Well, I'm trying to straighten out this missing painting situation."

"What about it? I understand Miss Johnson was arrested. My employee is going to have to make an ID."

I shrugged. "Doesn't make sense to me." He didn't respond. "I like things to make sense."

He went back to adjusting a painting. "Not everything does, Mr. Manning."

I nodded. I had long ago stopped trying to make sense of Kathleen. "I agree, but this is keeping me awake at night."

"That is a shame," he said with no concern for my sleep habits.

He wasn't good at sincerity. I continued without it.

"The police say you saw her take a painting."

"Not me. My employee."

I moved around in front of him. "And I don't doubt that. But I think she took a painting that wasn't supposed to be here in the first place."

He answered without looking at me. "That I know nothing about. There is a painting missing and she walked out with a painting. Simple logic."

"And which painting would that be?"

"That would be *Harbor Nights*."

I moved some more but he kept looking away. "I understand there was some confusion with the painting *Blue and Green*."

"Not as far as I know, Mr. Manning."

"Did you check the paintings when they arrived?"

"Do I look like I check in paintings? Now, if you will excuse me, I need to concentrate on my work."

"Sure, I can see you aren't at your best. Is your employee here?"

"Which employee would that be?"

"That would be the one who saw her walk out with a painting." I was working hard to be polite.

"Yes, but he's busy. We're working on your friend's show."

"I'd just like a few minutes."

"Well, perhaps if you come back this afternoon."

I nodded. "Okay. What's his name?"

"Tony Vitale."

"And your name is?"

He straightened his back with a haughty stance and looked me in the eye for the first time. "Mr. Bloom," he said, with the emphasis on the Mr.

"You're the owner, Mr. Bloom?"

"Hardly. I am the curator."

"And who is the owner?"

"I don't see where that is any of your business, Mr. Manning."

"When Tony said he saw Kathleen take the painting, you called the police and then checked the paintings you had?"

"Yes."

"And all thirteen were there. Correct?"

He looked nervous. "Well, we thought so. At least that's what I was told."

"Did you check the names?"

"No, Tony counted them."

"So nothing was stolen."

I could see tiny beads of sweat on his forehead and he appeared to be agitated. I continued.

"But the next day there was a missing painting."

"Yes."

"So couldn't it have been stolen after Kathleen left?"

He took a breath and tried to regain control. He didn't wipe off the sweat and still looked flustered.

"All I know is there was a missing painting and she was seen walking out with one. And you have taken up enough of my time."

"Well, thank you for sparing some." I didn't offer my hand.

He turned back to the painting and fiddled with the easel.

As I was walking out, he asked, "Do you know when?"

"When what?"

"When Tony is going to have to make the ID. I can't spare him for long."

"You'll have to talk to the police about that."

"I'll just do that," he said contemptuously. "It had better not take too long—that's all I can say." He had recovered his composure and his insolence.

I let myself out and walked back along the windows, glancing in. He was gone. I wondered if I had stirred another pot.

Chapter 14

parked on the street a few doors from Molly's a little before noon. A block from the station, it was a family restaurant serving breakfast and lunch and it was a popular police hangout. I nodded to several people I knew while looking around the diner. Rosie wasn't there. I sat near the door.

A few minutes before noon, a nervous-looking girl wearing a blue blazer came in and scanned the crowd. She walked slowly over to me.

"Are you Mr. Manning?" she asked hesitantly.

"I am. You must be Brenda."

She smiled. Brown, shoulder-length hair, brown eyes, a pug nose, and a nice smile. But overall, pretty homely.

"May I sit?"

I smiled back. "Of course." I held out my hand and she slid into the booth opposite me.

A waitress dropped off another glass of water. I told her we were expecting another and would order when she got there.

"Detective Lonnigan is going to be late," Brenda said nervously. She looked around the diner. "She said to entertain you." She barely smiled. "I'm not sure what that means."

There was something very odd about her voice. The words were kind of pinched off at the ends, almost like someone had their hands around her throat and squeezed a little whenever she talked. It sounded painful, but she didn't look like she was in any pain.

"Hmm. I can't wait to find out," I said with a slight smile.

"I'm also not supposed to take anything you say seriously."

"Nice. I'll have to have a talk with her."

She looked surprised. "Oh, no. That isn't from Detective Lonnigan, it's from…"

I held up my hand. "That's okay. I know who it's from."

We chatted for a half hour before Rosie showed up. Pitcher became more confident as she talked. She told me about growing up in a little town in southern Illinois and how she ended up as a cop on the streets of Chicago. I didn't quite follow the story, but it seemed like a big jump to me. But here she was, and her excitement about being a detective was obvious.

Rosie finally arrived, slid in next to me, and I caught the waitress' eye. Two Cokes and an iced tea for Brenda.

Looking at me suspiciously, Rosie asked Brenda, "Did he behave himself?"

With a laugh, Brenda replied, "Yes. We had a nice chat."

Rosie squinted at me with a smile. "Give him time."

"I stopped by Simmons," I said. "Met a guy named Bloom. Says he's the curator." I emphasized every syllable of the word.

The waitress dropped off the drinks and took our order.

Rosie took a long drink and, after chatting about the weather, asked if I had made any progress with Bloom.

I rolled my eyes. "That guy's a piece of work. Attitude from here to Door County."

"Tell me about it. I wish I had a reason to arrest him."

"Well, maybe I'll find one."

"Good luck."

"Did you get Cletis' address, Rosie?"

"Not yet. As soon as I get it I'll let you know."

"Thanks. I assume you haven't heard anything from up north."

She shook her head while chewing. The burger wasn't as good as Coyote's, but it was tasty. Hard to ruin a quarter pound of beef.

"What's your plan?" I asked.

"Not much." She wiped her mouth. "We're working on three other cases. A missing painting isn't going to get much attention."

"Sure." I didn't mention the missing person. I needed her on my side.

"And what's your next move?"

"Going back to Simmons this afternoon and talk to Tony. I'd like to get his take on the theft."

"His take is Kathleen took the painting."

"Yes, but which painting?"

"Good luck with that. He's cut out of the same cloth as Bloom, but not as refined."

"Sounds like fun."

We chatted some more as we finished eating. I asked Brenda if she looked forward to working with Steele. She said she would be happy to work with anyone. I wished her luck, paid for lunch, and left.

Chapter 15

I took a few hours to run errands and then headed back to Simmons around three. It had started to drizzle.

The bell rang again when I entered. This time a man came out of the back almost immediately. Slicked-back black hair, about six foot, pointy nose, and eyes too close together. I guessed mid-twenties. He wore dark slacks and a grey knit shirt. Evidently the dress code didn't require suits. I asked if he was Tony. He was.

"My name is Manning." I handed him a card.

"Yeah, I figured. The boss said you'd be coming back."

"I have a few questions."

"Doesn't mean I'll have any answers."

And I thought Bloom was bad.

"I understand you saw Kathleen Johnson walking out with a painting on Wednesday."

"Yup. I was just coming out of the back room when I saw her. She almost made it, but I caught her."

"What do you mean, she almost made it?"

"She was almost to the door. She almost got away with it."

I gave him my best perplexed look. "But she did get away with it. You didn't stop her."

He glared at me. "I don't mean the painting—I mean the crime. I saw her. I'm a witness."

"Ah, I see. Do you always leave the gallery unattended?"

"Oh, it isn't unattended. But we have a small staff. Sometimes we're in the back, working. But we come out to the front if the bell rings."

"So how did she have time to find the painting and almost get out with it unseen?"

"I remember being on the phone, and I was the only one here at the time. I got out as soon as I could."

I continued to press my point. "When I was at the gallery this morning, I was alone looking at paintings for a good five minutes. Then Mr. Bloom walked out and was startled to find me there. What about the bell?"

He acted a bit flustered and stuttered, trying to close the holes in his story. "Mr. Bloom is an old man—he doesn't hear so well."

I nodded. "Mr. Bloom said you were working in the back and couldn't talk to me. Didn't you hear the bell?"

More stuttering. "Well, I, I assumed Mr. Bloom would see to it. I was busy."

"Hmmm. And which painting was it you saw her take?"

"*Harbor Nights.*"

"Did you actually see the painting?"

He stared through me. I hadn't given him any reason to hate me, but his eyes said he did.

"I saw all I needed to."

"But did you see the painting?"

He started to walk away.

"What does 'all you needed to' mean?"

He turned around. "It means exactly that. Why don't you just mind your own business, Manning."

"Because minding your business is a lot more interesting. And your business just doesn't make sense, Tony. Kathleen had sent that painting down as part of the showing. Why would she take it?"

He shrugged. "Who the hell knows? That broad isn't all there."

I ignored the insult and kept my response to myself.

He turned and started to walk away again.

"Do you know Cletis Muddd?"

"Who?"

"Cletis Muddd. Three Ds."

He looked thoughtful and rubbed his chin. It looked almost sincere.

"No, can't say as I do. Now you have a nice day, Mr. Manning."

I replied before he could turn away. "Seems pretty strange, Tony, not to know somebody you've met." It also seemed strange that he didn't ask about the three Ds.

"And where would I have met this Cletis?"

"Mr. Bloom tells me you're the one who signed in the paintings from the frame shop."

"Yes, I was."

"Well, Cletis was the kid who delivered them."

His face lost the puzzled look. "That kid's name is Cletis?"

"It is."

"Strange name. Certainly would have remembered that if I had known."

I nodded. "Uh huh. But you *did* sign for the paintings, right?"

"Yes. Now I have to…"

"And how many paintings were shipped?"

"Well, the slip said thirteen."

"Not what I asked, Tony. Did you count them?"

He glanced to the side and clasped his hands in front of him. His eyes darted from side to side, never focusing on me.

"They were all in a large crate. There's never been a problem so I don't open the crate until we start to build the display."

"So there may have been fourteen, not thirteen?"

"I suppose. But why would there be fourteen?"

"Because Cletis made a mistake."

This time it was my turn to walk away. I let myself out, leaving him to wonder what was going on. As I reached the door, my pager vibrated. I found a phone and called Rosie, who gave me Cletis' Chicago address—3105 N. Kimball. Fifteen minutes away and not that much farther from the station.

***

3 105 Kimball was a four-story apartment building. Not the best on the block, but not the worst. There was a bell block inside the door. I rang the one labeled *Manager* and in a minute heard footsteps coming down the stairs. An old woman with a scarf on her head and wearing an ill-fitting dress, peered through one of the eye-level glass panes and opened the door a crack. She asked what I wanted.

I handed her a card and told her I needed some information about a prior tenant. She came out into the foyer and let the door close behind her.

"About three months ago there was a Cletis Muddd living here. Do you remember him?"

Her lips almost touched her nose as she scrunched up her face. Not a flattering move.

"You mean the one with the three Ds?"

I couldn't resist. "There was *another* Cletis?"

Nodding her head at an angle, she replied thoughtfully, like she wasn't sure. "No, he was the only one. We get a lot of tenants here, but never another one named Cletis."

"I bet not. Do you remember anything about him?"

"Like what, young man?"

I shook my head. "Like anything strange—how he behaved—did he pay his rent?—any trouble?"

"He paid his rent, not always on time, but it got paid. Not all do, you know. But I was glad to see him go."

"And why was that?"

"Caused a ruckus, those two. Lots of complaints about noise."

"Those two? He had a roommate?"

"Yup. Roommate is still here, but not as many complaints since the other fellow moved out."

"What's the roommate's name?"

"Tony, Tony Vitale."

I smiled big enough to cause the lady to ask why.

"I think I know Tony. Thanks for your time, ma'am. You've been very helpful."

She held out my card.

"Please keep it. Call me if you remember anything or if you ever need a private detective."

"We get evictions and I could throw some business your way."

"Sorry. I don't do evictions."

She shrugged and let herself back in with her key.

I was still smiling as I walked back to the car. Hard to forget your roommate, I'd think. So Tony had something to hide. I wondered what it was.

I had made plans to have dinner with Stosh. He had said he'd grill some steaks. I glanced at my watch and decided I had time to take a shower and headed home.

I pulled three days of mail out of the box next to the driveway and laid it on the dining room table. I wasn't good about checking mail, especially when I was working on a case.

There were two messages on the answering machine. One was from Paul, telling me there was still no sign of Cletis or Kathleen. The other was from Aunt Rose, who said she had some papers for me to sign and wondered when I was coming back. It had been two years since my folks had been killed and there was still red tape. They had been joint owners with Rose on several properties up in Door and had left them to me. I sighed, not happy about being reminded they were gone. I called and told Rose I'd be there by noon Tuesday.

Chapter 16

Stosh was sitting on the porch with a half-empty bottle of beer when I pulled into the driveway. "I see you started without me."

He didn't smile. "Tough day. You know where the fridge is."

I popped the cap off a bottle of Schlitz, started the grill, and went back to the living room. Stosh had moved to his recliner.

"So kid, what have you been up to?"

"Stirring some pots. Lighting a few fires to see what slimy creature crawls out."

"Yeah, great. One of your slimy creatures crawled into my office."

I gave him a sideways look in mid drink.

"Got a call from your Mr. Bloom. He wanted to know about his employee IDing the suspect."

I shrugged. "What's so hard about that?"

"He wasn't aware she had escaped."

I sat on the end of the couch. "Bet he wasn't happy."

"No." He set the bottle down. "Started lecturing me about the taxes he pays."

"Well, technically, he doesn't pay the taxes. He's just the manager, or rather curator."

"I didn't bring that up. So what were you doing at the gallery?"

"Stirring the pot."

He lifted the footrest and stretched out. "Why don't you go throw the steaks on the grill and get me another beer."

I put the steaks on, emptied a can of peas into a pot at low heat, and turned on the oven for tater tots. When I got back, his eyes were closed.

He didn't open them to say, "The gallery is out of the picture till we find Kathleen."

"I don't agree."

Folding back the footrest, Stosh stood up and said, "Of course not. Tell me about it after dinner. I want to eat in peace."

We ate in peace, not that talking about the Cubs' seven-game losing streak was peaceful. I washed the dishes. He dried and we returned to the same seats in the living room.

When he had settled in, he said, "Okay, whaddya got?"

I asked if Rosie had filled him in on the name confusion. She had. He wasn't too concerned.

"The kid up at the frame shop that shipped the paintings is missing. Didn't show up for work."

"Hard to get good help."

"Tony at Simmons signed in the paintings, but didn't check them—just assumed they were all there."

"And they were, right?"

"Yes. And I believe an extra one—*Blue and Green*. And that's the painting Kathleen took."

"Then why is *Harbor Nights* missing?"

I took a deep breath and let it out slowly. "Don't know—yet. But there's too many strange things here to think this is anything simple."

Stosh scoffed. "Don't see much strange besides the missing kid, and there's probably a simple explanation for that. Lots to do up there besides go to work."

"I asked Tony if he knew Cletis and he said he didn't. Then I reminded him he was the one who delivered the paintings. He said he never knew the kid's name."

Stosh shrugged. "So?"

"So, I stopped by Cletis' prior address over on Kimball. The manager told me she was glad to see the kid go cuz he and his roommate were pretty loud."

No response.

"Guess who the roommate was."

Stosh sat up. "Okay, more strange stuff. Gotta wonder why people lie."

I agreed. "If I keep stirring the pot I'm sure I'll find out."

"Well, we're pretty much done with this till Kathleen shows up. The missing kid is Ephraim's problem. Let me know if anything crawls out of your pot."

"Sure. And if you'll do me a favor... Bloom wouldn't tell me who the owner is. If you could find out, I'd appreciate it."

"Already did. Basically, it's a holding company in a string of holding companies. This one is MaxAMillion."

"No personal name?"

"I put Peters on it. It took him all day to strip away the layers. Does the name Larry Maggio ring any bells?"

"Larry Maggio the crime boss?"

"Yup."

"And you don't think something strange might be going on?"

"I don't think till I get facts, and so far we're short on facts."

"From what I hear, Maggio is pretty straight. Upstanding businessman, benefactor, sends old ladies fruit baskets at Christmas. Swell guy."

"That's the picture. And some of it is true. These days, they've traded goons with machine guns for lawyers with brief cases."

"Sure, less expense on bullets."

"But it costs them a lot more for lawyers than it did for goons. And you can't ignore the genes."

"What does that mean?"

"Does the name Torrio ring a bell? Johnny Torrio?"

"No. Should it?"

"Not necessarily. How about Capone?"

I laughed. "Don't be silly. Of course."

"Well, Johnny Torrio was the guy who started running moonshine in Chicago during prohibition. When he got tired of killing people, he turned the business over to his protégé, Al Capone. Al made him proud."

"So, what does that have to do with genes?"

"Johnny Torrio was Larry Maggio's grandfather."

"Nice. So the art gallery is a front for something."

He spread his hands. "Or money laundering."

"Stolen art would make the most sense."

"Not happy about your stirring this pot, Spencer."

"I'll stir carefully."

He turned and looked straight at me with a furrowed brow. "And if anything even starts to crawl out you're going to call me."

"Promise. I don't have a death wish."

He just nodded. "Anything else?"

"No. I'm going back to Door tomorrow. Aunt Rose has some papers for me to sign."

"Okay. Be careful. Let's play some gin."

By ten I was up three bucks.

Chapter 17

By noon Tuesday I was pulling into Aunt Rose's drive. Maxine was sitting in a rocker on the porch rubbing behind Amelie's ears.

"Tough duty, lady."

"All part of the job description. I grin and bear it."

She looked relaxed and as happy as anyone could. "I'll talk to Rose about the work conditions," I offered.

Her smile got bigger and she looked down at the cat. Amelie looked back with an attitude that said, *You can look, but don't bother me.*

As I walked up the steps, I asked, "What time do you get off?"

"I *am* off. Tuesdays and Wednesdays and whenever else we're not busy."

"Great! I have some stops to make this afternoon. You wanna come along and see some sights?"

"Sure. That'd be great!"

"Good. I'm gonna scare up some lunch. About an hour?"

"I'll be right here basking in the sun."

I made a ham sandwich, chatted with Aunt Rose about the Kathleen situation, and finished lunch with homemade cherry pie. I cleaned up and met her in her office where we sat at the desk and I signed six papers. She suggested I read them. I told her I trusted her and had better things to do.

"Spencer, you need to take these things more seriously."

With a serious look, I said, "I assure you, that was a very serious signature."

She shook her head and asked what my afternoon plans were.

"I have a few stops to make. Going to take Maxine and show her some sights."

"That's nice, but I want her back here in one piece."

"Yes, ma'am."

"I'm serious, Spencer. She's a wonderful girl. You should…"

"Now, Aunt Rose. I entirely agree about how wonderful Maxine is, and we're great friends. Period."

She straightened the pile of papers. "You could do a lot worse."

"Yes I could, and I probably will." I gave her a kiss on the cheek and told her not to wait up. She had said I could do worse than Kathleen and a *lot* worse than Maxine. I wondered if that put Maxine higher or lower on the scale than Kathleen. I couldn't decide.

***

My first stop was the Alpine Golf Resort to see Adam. Maxine waited in the car. His secretary smiled and told me to go in. I just wanted to see if he had any news. He didn't. I headed south on Highway 42.

"Where to next, Spencer?"

"Not too far. We're almost there."

"Almost where?"

"You'll see," I said mysteriously.

Six minutes later I pulled into a clearing at the edge of the forest.

Maxine looked at me with surprise—not *good* surprise, more like *what the hell?* surprise.

"See the sign up ahead?"

"Yes."

"It's a geographical marker. Forty-five degrees north latitude."

I got a blank stare.

"Forty-five degrees north."

"I got it. So what?"

"So what? Maxine—you're halfway to the north pole!"

She started to laugh. I gave her my best hurt look. I'd have to tell Aunt Rose about this flaw in her perfect girl.

"Spencer." She tried to talk in between laughs. "I'm sorry. I'm not laughing at you. It's just…" And she laughed harder.

It took a minute for her to calm down enough to ask if the next stop was to see Santa.

"Nice. I'm not telling you where the next stop is."

I turned around, and turned right onto County Highway E, and headed toward Bailey's Harbor. I pointed out the Coyote Roadhouse.

"So, really, where are we going?"

"Have you been to any of the lighthouses?"

"Rose took me to Eagle Bluff in the park."

I nodded. "Nice."

"And I climbed the tower in the park. The view is spectacular."

"Haven't been to Cana Island?"

"No. She said we'd go sometime."

"Well, sometime is now. Kathleen's best friend, Ginny, is the manager at the lighthouse. You'll like it."

"Any geographical markers?"

"Smart ass."

She laughed. This time it was light and very appealing.

As we turned into the forest onto County Q, I told her about the island and the lighthouse.

"We'll have to walk across a causeway to get to the island. When I was a kid the water was up to my knees. The lake is down so it might just be over your ankles now."

We wound around the curves on Q, and as we came up to a clearing I pointed out Moonlight Bay.

"Oh Spencer, that's beautiful. I can't imagine living in a place like this."

I agreed without telling her I *did* live there. Ten minutes later, I parked at the side of the road and we walked to the causeway.

"That's Lake Michigan to your left and another bay to your right." The lake was almost dead calm but could be deceiving. Many boaters who didn't check the forecast before going out found out the hard way. Dead calm could turn into stormy seas in a matter of minutes. I had seen twenty foot waves on this lake. Many boats and ships were on the bottom of the Great Lakes, the most famous being the Edmund Fitzgerald.

"Where's the lighthouse?"

"You'll see." It was hidden by the trees on the island.

We took off our shoes and socks and waded through the water to the tree-covered island. The path through the trees opened into a clearing with a clear view of the white tower.

Maxine stopped and stared with her mouth open. "Spencer, it's beautiful. How many are there up here?"

I answered as we walked up to the lighthouse. "There are eleven lighthouses in the county, most in any county in the country."

"Can we see some more?"

"We'll stop at another when we leave here." I held the door for her.

Ginny saw Maxine first, excitedly welcomed her, and started in on her spiel. Then she saw me and her face changed to a look heading toward terror.

"Oh, Spencer. I don't know anything!" Ginny said.

"Nice to see you, too, Ginny. What don't you know anything about?"

"About anything—that's what." She nervously looked at Maxine. Her eyes begged for help.

"Ginny, you've always been the worst liar in the world. Max, why don't you look through the store while I find out what Ginny doesn't know anything about. Then we'll climb the tower."

Maxine walked into the adjacent room.

Ginny started to follow her. "I should stay with the guests."

I moved between her and the doorway. "I promise she won't steal anything."

Ginny sighed and leaned on a counter.

"When did you see her, Ginny?"

Her lower lip quivered and her brow furrowed. "I don't want to get her in trouble."

"She's already in trouble. She escaped from the police. And if you know anything and don't tell, you'll be in trouble, too. I'm trying to help her, Ginny,"

Clasping her hands together, she said, "She was here Saturday morning. She was waiting in the woods and stopped me on the path when I got here."

"What time was that?"

"About eight-thirty."

"Didn't you see her car?"

"No. I asked her about that. She said she parked it in her uncle's garage not too far from here and walked through the woods."

"And?"

After a deep breath, she continued. "And, she told me someone had broken into her studio and was after her. She asked if she could stay in the basement."

"And you let her?"

"Well, not right away. I asked if she called the police."

I just looked at her.

"She said something strange. She said she didn't trust the police. And she said you'd be coming up."

"Did she say why she didn't trust them?"

She shook her head. Out of the corner of my eye I saw Maxine looking at a book rack.

"No. I asked, but she just said she needed a place to stay for the day."

"And you agreed?"

"I did. She made me lock the door to the basement and told me if anyone asked I didn't have the key. I suggested she call Adam, but she told me not to tell anyone."

"What did you think?"

She shrugged. "I didn't know what to think. I knew she had escaped—it was on the radio. But Kathleen can be, well, you know."

"Yeah, I know. So when did she leave?"

"When the last person had left, I opened the basement door. That was about five."

"And she walked out with you?"

"No. I was locking the door and talking to her. When I turned around, she was gone."

"Did you look for her?"

Maxine walked back into the room and looked at the wall displays.

Ginny shook her head. "I called her name, but she didn't answer. I figured she didn't want to be found, so I left."

"Did she say anything about what she was going to do?"

"When we were inside, I asked where she was going. She said there was something she needed to do. I don't remember exactly what she said, but she mentioned Grizzly."

I'm sure I didn't hide my surprise. I wanted to look around and asked if I could look in the basement. She gave me the key. I asked her if she'd take Maxine up the tower and told her I'd listen for the door.

Finding nothing unusual in the basement, I went outside and walked around the tower. I found nothing there either. As I came around to the front, a family with two kids walked into the clearing. I waited at the door, let them in, and told them the docent was giving a tour and would be down in a few minutes.

When Ginny got down, she told the people she would be right with them and took me aside. In a quiet voice, she asked, "Should I call the police?"

"No. If anything comes of this you may be questioned later, but for the moment let's keep this quiet."

She sighed and looked relieved.

I found Maxine on the beach, which was mostly rocks, and suggested we leave and get some food. It was almost six. I told her about my conversation with Ginny and that we were going to make a stop at Kathleen's uncle's place about five minutes down the road.

"Do you think her car is still there?"

"We'll find out. If she *was* there, she's probably gone by now."

The house was a two-story log cabin set back in the woods a few hundred feet. There was a *No Trespassing* sign at the entrance to the drive. No one was home, but Kathleen's car was in the garage. I stuck my card in the crack between the front door and the jamb with a note to call me.

When I got back in the car, I told Maxine what I had found.

She looked like she had questions but didn't ask any.

Chapter 18

had planned to have dinner at the Greenwood Supper Club, a wonderful steak house in the peninsula's interior that few tourists know about. On the weekends it's packed with locals. They don't take reservations, but I figured Tuesday wouldn't be too busy.

I told Maxine we'd stop on the way and look at the Bailey's Harbor range lights across the street from the harbor. I explained that the purpose of range lights was to show boaters out on the lake where the center of the channel was into the harbor. In this case, there was a front red light at the top of a small, wooden tower and a rear white light in the cupola of an old building that looked like a schoolhouse. The rear light was higher than the front. Boaters had to move to a point where the two lights lined up and that would be the course they needed to follow into the harbor.

"The range lights were lit in 1869. This was an important logging town back then and the state highway that runs through town wasn't built until 1870. So the harbor was pretty valuable to commerce."

I parked at the side of the road and we walked down a wooden walkway that led through the woods to the rear building.

I put out my hand and stopped her. I pointed off to our left where a doe was staring at us from the protection of the trees.

"Wow," Maxine whispered.

The doe turned and slowly walked into the woods. We continued along the walkway.

I pointed to a sign off to the right. "That's a path into the Ridges Sanctuary. It's a bog that's a wildflower conservatory. You'll find somewhere around twenty-five species of native orchids."

"Up here?"

"Yup. Nature is amazing. You should come over sometime and walk through—it's beautiful."

We checked out the building and then headed back. About halfway back to the car, Maxine said, "This would be a great spot for someone to hide."

I laughed. "It would, but there are many more that are better, and with room and board. The county is full of Johnsons, most of whom are relatives of Kathleen."

She laughed.

***

We headed back into town and turned onto County Highway F toward Greenwood. On the way she asked who Grizzly was. I made a mental note about Maxine's excellent hearing.

"Grizzly is an old fellow up on Washington Island. He's been there forever—must be in his eighties. He lives in a cabin with no electricity or running water. Still has an outhouse. And he's somehow related to Kathleen—great uncle or something."

"Really? No electricity? In today's world? Is he poor?"

I chuckled. "That depends on how you measure it. He has very few possessions, but his cabin sits on one hundred ten acres. He leases out a lot of it to farmers who raise various crops. I'm guessing he's worth millions."

She was quiet for a minute. "You have to get there by ferry, right?"

"Right."

"I'm thinking an island is a bad place to hide," she said thoughtfully. "Why narrow down the places someone has to look?"

I had been thinking about that and had come to the same conclusion. "I agree. But there's another piece to the puzzle. Grizzly has very few things, but one of them is a boat, and there are other islands to hide on."

"Can she drive a boat?"

"Yup. But it's more than knowing how to drive." We followed F as it took a turn to the left. "You have to know these waters—especially up there. The county gets its name from the waters between the tip of the peninsula and Plum Island, the first island to the north. That area is called Death's Door because of the boaters who learned the hard way."

Maxine commented on the scenery as we passed orchards and small farms.

"Are you going to see Grizzly?"

"Yup. Do you want to come?"

"Sure. But it would have to be tomorrow."

"Tomorrow it is."

I pulled into the parking lot across from Greenwood and took Maxine's hand as we crossed the street. We got a table right away and we both ordered steaks.

Maxine looked puzzled.

"Something on your mind?" I asked with a smile.

She took a deep breath. "Well, if she was going up to the island, why would she leave her car in the garage?"

"Good question. The ferry registers cars but not people. If she didn't want to leave a trail she wouldn't take her car."

"So how would she get to the ferry?"

"Lots of options. Any number of friends and relatives who would give her a ride to the island."

"Help an escaped prisoner?"

I laughed. "Those relationships go pretty far up here. Help a friend get away from a big-city cop? I bet they'd be standing in line."

She laughed. "So you just have to find out who."

"Not even going to try. Too many possibilities. If she went to the island, it doesn't matter how she got there."

I took a drink of beer and asked how the job was going. She gave me a huge smile and talked through most of the meal. She was in heaven.

I listened to her, but didn't respond much as I tried to sort out the pieces of the puzzle. I still didn't have enough pieces.

Chapter 19

The sun had set by the time we were done, but it was still warm enough to not need a jacket. There was a heat wave coming in the next few days. Temperatures were supposed to reach 90 by Thursday. I don't mind the heat, but I've never been happy about the humidity that comes with it up here. When I was a kid, we didn't have air conditioning, and I spent many nights on the porch, in the hammock, trying to catch the breeze.

I held the door for Maxine and asked if she was willing to make one more stop.

"Sure. Where?"

"I'd like to stop by the frame shop."

"At this time of night?"

"I'd just like to take a look in the window."

"Fine with me."

We turned left on Highway 42, headed back toward Fish Creek, and parked on the street across from Framed. The lights were out but the *Open* sign was still in the window. The door wasn't locked. That seemed strange, and strange things were usually not good.

I wished I had my gun with me, but I didn't like carrying it around. Just too inconvenient.

I asked Maxine to wait outside and went in.

The place had been torn apart—just like Kathleen's studio. I turned on the light and walked into the back room. It also was a mess. Whatever was going on was a lot bigger than Kathleen. I wondered how she was tied to it. It must have something to do with the painting.

I pushed a broken frame out of the way with my foot and walked around the corner of the workbench. A leg was sticking out. It was attached to Edvard Gunderson. I bent down. There was no pulse and his skin was cold. His head lay in a pool of drying blood.

I walked outside and asked a worried-looking Maxine to find a phone and tell the Ephraim police there was a body inside Framed.

I went back in and took another look at Gunderson. The blood had come from the right side of his head. There were scratches and bruises on his face and neck. Somebody was still looking for something and they were willing to kill to get it. I looked for a murder weapon. There were several tools around, but none with blood on them. Power woodworking tools were sitting on the long table. There was a crosscut saw, a small band saw, a joiner for corners, and a small drill with a bit in the chuck. I took a few steps toward the door and then stopped and looked at the drill. Why would a framer need a drill? Partially built frames were scattered on one bench.

There were three benches. One was bare. Another was a surprise. There were more tools on top, but these were carving knives of various sizes. There were also paints and brushes. Also on top were the objects someone had been carving—duck decoys. Several were partially carved, and one was painted. The workmanship was exquisite. I wondered if it had been carved by Gunderson or Cletis.

Paul pulled up five minutes later with Chief Iverson right behind him. Paul went in while I waited at the door for the chief. He put on his cap as he got out of the squad car.

The chief glanced at Maxine as he walked up. "So we meet again, Manning."

I just nodded.

"Trouble still following you around?"

I didn't respond and started to follow him into the store.

He put up his hand and said, "Why don't you just wait out here? This is police business."

I waited.

"What did you do to *him*?" Maxine asked.

I shrugged. "Just showed up, I guess. Don't let his gruff manner fool you—we're really great buddies."

She nodded. "I could tell. Do you think your great buddy will want your help?"

I pointed toward a bench in front of the store and we sat down. "I'm guessing that's the last thing he'd want."

A crowd had started to gather across the street.

"Good guess," Max said. "Do you think your friend is involved in this?"

I shook my head. "She must be, but I can't see how. I'm thinking it has something to do with her painting. That's the common thread. It was here at the frame shop, and down at the gallery, and then supposedly back here after Kathleen took it."

Maxine turned sideways on the bench. "But where is it now?"

"Good question."

Chief Iverson reappeared at the door.

"What time did you get here, Manning?"

I looked at my watch. "About twenty-five minutes ago, a little after ten."

"And how did you get in?"

"The door was open. I *walked* in," I said with an obvious disrespectful edge.

He gave me a skeptical look. "Yeah, all of our merchants just leave their doors open after business hours."

"Meaning?"

"Meaning too many things are happening since you arrived." His look was not friendly.

I kept my thoughts to myself.

"Who's the lady?"

"Her name is Maxine. She works at the Harbor Lantern Inn."

He nodded to her. "Were you in the store, ma'am?"

She shook her head, no.

"Why did you come here, Manning?"

"Still looking for the kid, Cletis. I assume you haven't heard from him."

He pointed his finger at me. "Seems to me who I've heard from and who I haven't is none of your business. Also seems to me you know more about this than you're telling. I don't like that. It didn't concern me as much when it was a missing person, but this looks like murder. You sit right down there on the bench while I come up with some reason for locking you up."

I sat down. "You've got to be kidding. I *called* you."

"Yeah, perfect cover. You said the door was unlocked, right?"

"Right."

He rubbed his chin and slowly shook his head. "I have a problem with that. Yes, I do. It just doesn't make sense. Some guy comes in, kills Gunderson, searches the place, and then leaves the door open so anyone can walk in and find him. Me? I'm locking the door so the guy isn't found till the next day. You got an explanation for that—I mean other than you picked the lock?"

"I already told you what happened. Maybe something scared the murderer away."

The words I almost said next would have given him his reason to lock me up. Maybe that's what he was hoping. Maxine squeezed my leg and I kept quiet.

"Gruber!"

"Yeah, Chief."

"Get out here and keep an eye on this guy." Paul came out and the chief went in.

I looked at Paul with dismay. His eyes got wide and he shrugged. I beckoned him over to the bench.

"What do you know about this guy, Paul?"

"Come on, Spencer, the *guy* is just inside there," whispered Paul.

"Can you be at Al's at eight thirty? Breakfast is on me."

"I'll be there."

Chief Iverson came back out. "Do you plan on leaving anytime soon, Manning?"

"Don't know." I stood up and pulled Maxine up off the bench. "You plan on doing anything to find Cletis?" We started toward the street.

He pulled down his cap. "I wouldn't leave town if I were you. You're hiding something and I intend to find out what it is."

"Good luck with that, Iverson."

"That's Chief Iverson, punk."

I stopped at the curb and turned back to him. "I'll make you a deal. You start acting like one and I'll call you one." I didn't wait for a response and I didn't look back.

I headed north on 42. It took ten minutes to get back to the inn. Neither of us said anything until I had parked and turned off the car.

Maxine turned toward me with a playful smile. "You've got a lotta guts for a guy three hundred miles from home."

"Hey. I can be just as much of a pain in the ass at home."

She laughed and then quickly turned serious. "He doesn't like you."

"Nope. And I'm wondering why."

"Maybe he feels threatened. You're an out-of-town guy coming into his territory."

"He *should* feel threatened. Appears he's not doing his job."

She rolled up her window and opened the door. "Maybe he is. Maybe he's just not telling *you* about it."

I grimaced. "I've heard that before. Could be. But the way he goes about it is pretty strange. And Ginny told me Kathleen didn't call the police because she didn't trust them."

"Didn't trust who?"

"Well, Ginny didn't say and probably didn't ask. But I'm going to assume Kathleen trusts her cousin Paul. That only leaves Iverson."

"You think he's involved in this?"

I pursed my lips and thought for a few seconds. "No, I just wonder how well he's doing his job."

"Because of what Kathleen said?"

"Not entirely. I take things she says with a grain of salt. But something sparked her to say it, and my own experience with him just makes me wonder. I don't trust him. It's worth keeping an eye on him."

Maxine got out and leaned back in. "What time are you picking me up for breakfast?"

I rubbed the steering wheel with two fingers. "I don't know if that's a good idea, Maxine. This has gotten serious. Gunderson didn't slip and hit his head."

"Come on, Spencer. I'm not afraid of danger—remember where I used to live?"

I sighed. "Sure, but this is murder."

Another playful smile. "And do you recall what brought us together? Let me think. Oh yeah, a murder. Across the hall if I remember correctly. This isn't even in the same town."

I turned on the car. "Okay, I know when I'm beat. Pick you up at eight-fifteen."

"I'll be on the porch. Thanks for the dinner and the tour, Spencer. I had a good time."

"My pleasure, Max—me too."

I watched her walk up to the porch feeling like I was missing something. A good night kiss would have been nice. She turned and waved as I backed out.

On the way back to Moonlight Bay I should have been thinking about the case, but found myself thinking about Maxine. This wasn't a date, it was just two friends enjoying an evening. Our dinner in Chicago hadn't been a date either. I had enjoyed both and, as I pulled into the horseshoe drive in front of the cottage, I decided I would like to have a first real date with Maxine. But that would probably never happen.

I sat on the deck, looking at the stars and listening to an owl. When it stopped hooting, I went to bed.

Chapter 20

Paul was waiting for us when we pulled into the parking lot of Al Johnson's Swedish Restaurant in Sister Bay. I waved and held up a finger. Maxine wanted to go look at the goats. The food at Al's was great, especially breakfast—everything cherry you could ever want. But Al was famous for the goats on the sod roof. Hard to get a lawnmower up on a roof. The tradition had come over from Europe where sod roofs were common, homes were built into the sides of hills, and the goats could just stand up there and graze.

Maxine was enthralled. "I wonder how all this started."

"The story is that Al had a friend who gave him crazy presents every year. One year it was a goat with red ribbons tied on his horns. He thought it would be a great idea for Al to have goats on the roof. So he carried the goat up a ladder, placed it on the roof, and promptly fell off the roof, breaking a few ribs."

Maxine laughed. "I would have loved to have seen that. I hope somebody took movies."

We walked back around the front of the building where Paul was waiting on a bench.

I officially introduced them and the hostess gave us a friendly welcome and showed us to a table.

"Nice seeing you last night, Paul. We'll have to do it more often."

He shook his head with a look of relief. "I was sure I'd be giving you breakfast in bed this morning on the county. You swim with sharks often?"

I laughed. "I've been known to ruffle feathers at times. Diplomacy isn't my strong point."

"I noticed."

"I'll take some crap when I have to, but there's a line."

"Nice to have that option. If I want a job I have to take his crap. Lots of *yes sirs*."

"The guy seems pretty incompetent. What do you know about him?"

"Not much. I haven't had any reason to ask questions. He hired me. That's all I needed to know."

The waitress brought juice and coffee.

"Do you get along with him?" asked Maxine.

Taking a sip of coffee, he answered, "Sure. No reason not to. I do my job and go home."

"No problems?" I asked.

He chuckled. "Hey. This ain't Chicago. This may be the first murder we've ever had. Our worst problems are traffic issues."

"So, maybe he doesn't know how to do his job."

"Don't know. He knows enough to please the mayor."

"And maybe that's usually all he needs. But this is certainly different from a speeding ticket. Two missing persons, and a murder and a missing painting."

Paul pursed his lips. "Well, technically the painting is Chicago's problem, and the sheriff is looking for Kathleen and has taken over the murder."

"How hard do you think they're looking for Kathleen?"

"After last night? Not at all. Before then, maybe a little, but it wasn't a priority."

"And how about Cletis? I suggested that Iverson should be looking for him—twice. And I don't get an answer. Doesn't seem too competent."

"Ah. Well, just because he doesn't answer doesn't mean he isn't doing something."

Maxine laughed with a sparkle in her eye and a *told you so* in her attitude.

"That's enough, lady."

I turned back to Paul. "Are you saying he *is* doing something?"

"Well, not exactly, but he told *me* to do something. Gunderson has a boat. We went through his house and found a key peg rack in the kitchen. The one marked boat was empty. I checked the marina and his boat is gone. The kid on duty didn't remember anything about it. I asked people in the slips on his dock and no one remembers seeing him there recently or seeing the boat leave. A few did say the boat was there over the weekend."

Our food arrived. "If the kid did kill Gunderson and take the boat we can narrow it down once we get the coroner's report."

"We?"

I took a bite of bacon. Maxine was busy eating. I laughed. "Sorry. Habit. You, I mean. And if you'd let me know, I'd appreciate it. In the meantime, I sure wish I knew where that kid is. Could you check other harbors for the boat?"

"Already done. Chief had me do that, too. I called the Coast Guard in Sturgeon Bay last night. They notified all the harbors and Milwaukee issued a UMIB, an urgent marine information broadcast. Periodic messages are sent out with the boat description and ID number. So there are lots of people looking."

I soaked up some egg with a piece of toast. "Chief did all that, did he?"

"Yeah. Must've been while he was taking a break from being incompetent."

"I get it. But he could be nicer to the public."

"He *is* nice to the public. It's big city cops and P.I.s he's not crazy about. And it's hard to blame him."

"It is?" I asked, taking another bite of bacon.

"Yeah. It wasn't him that lost Kathleen."

"I'll give him that." I scooped up the last bite of pancake. "Another question for you."

"Shoot."

"I heard through the grapevine that Kathleen doesn't trust the police. Any idea why?"

"Trust? No. But she's not too happy with us. A few months ago someone egged her windows. Probably high school kids. No one was caught and she made it clear that she thought we weren't doing all we could to find the culprit."

"I bet she did. But that wouldn't cause a trust issue. Do you have any idea when we might get an answer from the coroner?"

"No. But my guess would be a few days. The body went to the medical examiner in Green Bay. They cover a lot of territory."

"Would you let me know?"

"Sure. I'll leave a message on your machine."

"Thanks, Paul. You done, Maxine?" I really didn't have to ask. There was nothing left on her plate.

"Yup. That'll hold me till dinner."

They both thanked me for breakfast. Paul headed south. We took Highway 42 north to the tip of the peninsula.

"Spencer, mind if I throw in my two cents?"

"Of course not."

She turned toward me in the bucket seat. "Let's go back to Kathleen not trusting the police. Are you sure it's not Paul?"

I took a deep breath and turned left at the junction with Highway 57. "Yeah, I was interested in his reaction as well as his answer. Nothing strange about either one. I can't imagine this would be about Paul, but you never know."

"And do you feel better about the chief?"

I laughed. "Partly. Still not so thrilled about his bedside manner."

"Yeah, pretty gruff. I wonder why."

We were both silent as we followed the winding road through the forest. This was one of my favorite parts of the peninsula. I felt like I was the only car on the road as we wound through the majestic cedar trees and pines that lined both sides.

Chapter 21

The ferry was loading when we drove out of the forest at the end of the road. I paid as the attendant wrote my car and license plate on the manifest. I pulled in behind a Chevy wagon. We got out and stood at the rail. A warm wind was blowing from the southwest. Put that together with the moisture up here and that meant humidity, and storms.

"How long is this trip?" asked Maxine.

"About a half hour."

She put her arm through mine and said, "Add this to my list of firsts because of Spencer Manning."

I squeezed her arm.

The channel between the islands was a bit choppy thanks to the wind. I asked Maxine how her stomach was doing.

"Fine." She pointed to the northeast. "Is that the island?"

"No. That's Plum. Washington is much bigger. You can see part of it off to the left."

"Do people live there?"

"Yup, a permanent population of about six hundred."

She let go of my arm. "Permanent? Even in the winter?"

"Yup."

"How do they get things?"

"Well, the ferry runs into December. After that they use snowmobiles after the ice forms."

She just stared at the island. "This is certainly a different life. I never could have imagined all this before you brought me up here. These islands are a totally different experience from Ephraim. And Cana Island is different again." She looked thoughtful as she gazed out over the waters of Death's Door. "Someone who lives up here doesn't have to leave the county to take a vacation. They just have to drive twenty minutes and they're in a whole new world."

"I agree. This is a wonderful place." I was impressed by Maxine's thoughts and feelings and felt very close to her. I wanted to put my arm around her, but didn't.

"What's your plan once we get there?" she asked.

"To visit Grizzly. Then we can drive around a bit—I'll give you the nickel tour."

We docked and I took County W north to Townline Road. Grizzly lived on the other side of the island in a small log cabin that he had helped build a long time ago. Townline ran straight east. The land on both sides was either forest or farmland. There weren't many homes. Ten minutes later, I turned left onto a dirt road that went straight north through a forested area. A cloud of dust kicked up behind the Mustang. The cabin was visible when we cleared the trees.

Grizzly was chopping wood in front of the porch.

As I rolled to a stop, Maxine said, "Interesting-looking fellow."

"Yup. In many ways."

Grizzly glanced briefly in our direction and went back to chopping. Long gray hair pulled into a pony tail and a gray beard betrayed his age. But his muscular arms and chest took off twenty years. He stopped and leaned on the axe as we walked up.

"Hello, Grizzly. You won't remember me, but…"

"Runny-nosed kid, asked questions about everything. Good eye with a rifle. How ya doin' kid?"

I laughed as Maxine stood with her mouth open.

"Doin' great, Grizzly. And you don't look a day older."

He squinted and eyed me closely. "Always figured some of the things that came out of your mouth were lies. You've added a pretty girl since I saw you last." He looked at Maxine with reverence.

I introduced her.

He bowed slightly. "Pleased to meet you ma'am. Please pardon my working duds."

He turned back to me. "Is your old man still a cop?"

"No. He was killed a few years ago."

"Aw, geez, that's tough, kid. My sympathies to you and your mom."

"Thanks. But she was killed, too."

He shook his head. "Hard to find words for all that."

"Thanks. I appreciate it."

"You a cop, too?"

"No. I thought about it but went the private investigator route."

He buried the axe in a stump and laughed. "That figures. Still asking a lot of questions, eh? So what brings you to Chez Grizzly?" He grinned and swept an arm across the front yard.

"Trying to find Kathleen."

He invited us up to the porch and pointed to log chairs.

"It's a long, confusing story, but she's missing. She escaped from two detectives and disappeared."

He nodded and scratched at his cheek. "And you think she's here?"

I gazed off at the trees. "I always loved this land, Grizzly. What a beautiful place to live."

We were all quiet for a few minutes.

"I don't have many facts, but this is a possibility," I said with some hesitation.

"Well, she's not."

I nodded. "When was the last time you saw her?"

He rubbed his beard. "Not since last year. She always comes up at the end of the year to see if I need anything. I never do, but it's nice to see her."

I nodded again. "Don't you want to know why she was with detectives?"

"Nope. None of my business. I figure you would have told me if you wanted me to know."

He had been looking at Maxine, who was staring out at the property. He turned to me and asked, "So is there something that makes you think she came here?"

"Yeah. Thought she might want to borrow your boat."

"Well, if she did, she didn't ask. You're welcome to go down to the boat-house and see if it's there."

"Thanks, I'll do that." I looked around some more. "You know, this place doesn't change. The trees are bigger and your beard might be longer, but I feel like I just walked in fifteen years ago. You're still living by your rule."

He smiled, looking peaceful and content.

Maxine looked confused. "What rule is that?"

He looked thoughtful as he gazed out over his yard. "The land has a big effect on me and I have little effect on it. I built this here cabin and dug a hole for the crapper, but that's about it. Grow some crops. I take care of it and it takes care of me."

"That's wonderful, Grizzly," said Maxine. "I used to live in a place where all kids had was a sidewalk to play on. They'll never ever see something like this."

He shook his head. "That's a real shame, ma'am."

She looked strangely at me.

"What's the matter, Maxine?"

"Well, I, uh…"

"Spit it out, young lady," Grizzly said with a sparkle in his eye.

"Okay, if you don't mind, I'd, well, I've never seen an outhouse."

We all started to laugh. He was one happy old man.

He stood up, offered his arm, and they headed around to the back of the cabin.

Maxine looked over her shoulder. "Aren't you coming?"

"No, I'll pass. I've seen the outhouse. Not one of my fondest memories. Grizzly, if you don't mind, I'll drive over to the boathouse and leave you with Maxine."

"If I don't mind? I'm old—I'm not dead!"

They walked off laughing, her arm linked through his.

I got back forty-five minutes later. They weren't back yet so I sat in the rocker and fell asleep listening to the birds. More laughter woke me up a half hour later.

"Did you enjoy the outhouse?"

"I did," she said, excitedly. "Along with everything else. He showed me where fawns were born, a spring that I took a drink from, rare flowers that only grow here, and so much more." She turned and gave Grizzly a hug. "Thanks so much, Grizzly. I love it here."

"Well, come back sometime and spend the night. The stars are amazing."

"I'll do that. But how will I know if you're here?"

Grizzly and I both laughed.

"Well, young lady, I'm always here. I have no reason to leave."

She looked aghast. "You mean you've never been off of this island?"

"Oh, I have, but I learned my lesson. When I was a bit younger, I used to go over to the mainland for fun. But I soon found out what they considered fun wasn't all that important."

Then his face changed and I thought I saw sadness. After a minute, he continued.

"And there was a woman once. But she couldn't get used to living out here without the modern conveniences."

Maxine touched his arm. "That's sad, Grizzly. I'm sorry."

"No reason to be sorry, young lady. We all make choices. Hers just didn't match mine. And I have come to learn that living with the land here is worth more to me than living with the wrong woman." Then his eyes twinkled and he put his arm around her waist. He leaned in toward her and said quietly, "But if you want to stay for a spell, I won't be kicking you out." He winked at me.

Maxine and I laughed. Grizzly smiled but he wasn't laughing. I thought there was still a hopeful look in those old eyes.

He turned to me. "Was the boat there, kid?"

I stood and walked down the steps to where they were standing and took a deep breath.

"No, it wasn't." I couldn't read his look.

"Kinda surprised she'd take it without asking. I wouldn't have said no."

"Well, maybe she didn't have time to ask, or maybe she's protecting you."

He looked surprised. "Protecting me? From what?"

"Somebody trashed her studio and the owner of a frame shop in Ephraim was murdered."

"Whooee. That sure is somethin'. I wonder when she took it."

"My guess would be Sunday or Monday."

He pulled at his beard. "And why."

"Damned good question. If I knew that maybe I could find her."

"Good luck with that, kid. I'll keep a good thought. Let me know."

"Thanks, Grizzly. Will do. Nice to see you again. Thanks for taking care of Maxine."

"My pleasure, kid. Don't let so much time go by."

"Will do."

Maxine waved as we drove away. "What a sweet man."

"Yeah. You won't find a better one."

She looked at me with a playful smile. "I might argue with you on that."

Taking a deep breath, I responded slowly. "Well, you're entitled to your opinion." I kept my eyes on the road but could feel her looking at me. "We'll stop at the grocery store and get a sandwich."

I parked on the dirt next to the store. We went inside, ordered ham sandwiches, and ate at a picnic bench next to my Mustang. Two more cars pulled up while we were eating.

"There's something that's bothering me," Maxine said.

"Shoot."

"I think Grizzly might know where she is."

"Why do you think that?"

"Well, he wasn't at all concerned about losing the boat. Kinda like he knew where it was."

I laughed. "Good catch, but not true. Two things about Grizzly. One, he doesn't lie—ever. If he says he hasn't seen her, he hasn't. Two, he doesn't care about the boat."

"That's hard to believe."

"For you and me. But not for Grizzly. Things just tie you down. If you have something that's going to bother you if you lose it, you never really enjoy it in the first place."

She looked confused. "I don't understand."

"If you have something valuable, you're buying insurance, or a safe, or whatever. You're spending time protecting it, not enjoying it."

She was quiet for a minute. "Do you believe that?"

"In theory, sure. Makes sense. But not so easy to do."

"But how did she get the key?"

"He leaves it in the boat—under the seat or maybe even in the ignition."

"Really? Makes it easy to steal."

I laughed. "Different life up here, Maxine. And pretty isolated. People don't lock their doors. And the boat is in a little cove. If you didn't know it was there you wouldn't know it was there. This way, his friends can borrow the boat without bothering him for the key."

We finished eating.

"Well, Spencer, you still haven't found her, but at least you know where she's been. Any ideas why she took the boat?"

"Nope. There's something she's doing. Wish I knew what."

We got back in the car and I turned away from the harbor and gave Maxine the tour. We made a brief stop at a wonderful little museum in a log cabin and ended at Schoolhouse Beach, a beach with no sand. The beach was entirely small limestone rocks rounded by the waves. We made the loop and headed back to the ferry.

As we turned right onto the harbor road, she said, "This all is pretty frustrating. Do you like doing this, Spencer?"

I pulled around a slow van. "Well, as Grizzly said, I like asking questions. But yes, sometimes it is frustrating. But you ask enough questions and there are usually answers."

"That doesn't answer my question."

"No, it doesn't. Yes, I like it a lot. I love solving puzzles and I sure like the freedom of not having to go to an office every day and punch a time clock."

"Do you always get the bad guy?"

"So far." I pulled onto the loading ramp. This time we were near the front. But that's only because I haven't done it much. The police aren't so lucky. But they have more than one case to work on."

"And from what I've seen, you're not getting rich on this."

I turned off the car and waited for the ferry. "What do you mean?"

"When you met me you were helping a little girl. She couldn't have had money to pay you. And this time you're helping your friend who you haven't even talked to."

I chuckled. "You are correct. But I'm lucky enough not to have to worry about it. My folks left me enough money to last the rest of my life."

She didn't respond for a minute and then reached out and touched my arm. "That must be hard, Spencer. If you ever want to talk..."

"Thanks, Maxine. I appreciate it." I lifted my arm and pointed out into the harbor. The ferry was coming. I would have loved to talk more, but mostly what I wanted to talk about was her.

Chapter 22

When I got home, I called Paul and asked him to get out another UMIB on Grizzly's boat. Then I put a burger on the grill. A bottle of Schlitz was already half empty.

The daytime temperature had reached ninety-four and the humidity had risen throughout the day. But the natural air conditioning of the woods next to Moonlight Bay kept the temperature down. The thermometer on the deck read 78.

I ate slowly and thought about Maxine. I had very much enjoyed spending the last two days with her. Taking her hand when we crossed the street to Greenwood had been a natural response and I liked it. I liked when she touched me and I liked that she thought I was special. And normally I would be thinking about making love with her. But I was pretty sure that would never happen. I had met her on a case and at that time she was making a living as a prostitute. If we ended up in bed, I was sure she would end up wondering what I was thinking and if I was having second thoughts. I wouldn't be, but I would always think she would think I was. And that would never be a good thing. So I raised my bottle to Maxine and called Stosh to see if he had anything new on the case.

***

Hi, Spencer. Where are you?"
"Still up in Door."

"Are you coming back anytime soon?"

"Yes. Tomorrow, but not sure why I ever leave here. You have anything new?"

"Nope. Do you?" asked Stosh.

"Mostly just a lot of frustration." I told him about Gunderson.

"Well, nice chatting with you. Thanks for calling," he said sarcastically.

"Yeah, good. Don't you want to hear about the frustration?"

"Not especially. I've got my own, but I leave it on my desk. Then you call and think I wanna hear yours. I take it you still don't know where Kathleen is."

"No. But I know several places where she isn't and a couple where she was." I told him about the boat.

"Makin' progress. Hang on a second."

I rearranged the pillows on the couch and stretched out. I heard him pick up the phone.

"So, there's a body in the morgue and a missing person. You think this is about the painting?"

"To some extent, yes. But to what extent I have no clue. It seems to be what started all of this, but there has to be more to it than just an attempt to steal her favorite painting."

"I agree. Have you talked to Rosie?"

"No. Has she mentioned me?"

"Just to ask if I've heard from you."

"How's the new detective doing?"

"Pitcher? Okay. No complaints."

"Is she working with Steele?"

"Sort of. Steele and Lonnigan are working separate cases, so Pitcher spends time with each."

"Does she get to choose who she likes best?"

"No, I get to. That's why I get the fancy desk."

"And the big paycheck. I'd like a favor."

"Of course you would. I'll send you a bill at the end of the month."

"There's a Chief Iverson up in Ephraim. Would you use your unofficial channels and see what you can find out about him?"

"You gonna tell me why?"

"No good reason. He's not real cooperative and doesn't seem to like me."

"So what's to look into? Sounds like he's got things figured out pretty well. Anything in particular?"

"You mean other than trying to think of some reason to arrest me?"

"I've been trying to think of a reason to arrest you for two years."

"Funny. But I'm serious. There's something odd up here. Kathleen told her friend she didn't call the police because she doesn't trust them."

"From what you've told me, your *friend* is a little odd, so maybe it's not the police."

"Maybe. But wouldn't hurt to check."

"So says you. Gotta go. Late game out in San Fran."

"Okay. I'll stop by tomorrow. I'll take the third inning."

"You're on."

We hung up and I decided to turn in and get an early start in the morning. Cubs and Giants. We always bet on what inning Stosh would fall asleep.

Chapter 23

I woke up early Thursday morning to the rumble of thunder, loaded my bag in the car before the rain started, and fried some eggs. I always hated leaving and thought maybe I'd buy a little business or hang out my shingle up here. But with the lack of crime, things might be pretty slow. That might not be all that bad, though—there was a lot of nothing I could do up here. Except for an accident before Green Bay, the drive was uneventful. The rain stopped just north of Milwaukee, but the sky stayed gray all the way home.

I pulled into the garage, dropped my bag in the kitchen, and figured I'd get a shower before lunch. The red light on the answering machine was flashing three times. I thought it was nothing that couldn't wait until after a shower.

I was wrong.

***

The first two messages were from prior clients. One said a check was in the mail and the other wanted to hire me again. Another happy customer. The third message started as I got the roast beef out of the fridge. I dropped the beef on the counter, closed the fridge, and replayed the message: *We've got your girlfriend, Manning. If you want her back, we can make a trade. We'll call back with instructions.*

No wonder we couldn't find Kathleen. The message had been left this morning. I wondered how long they'd had her. And what did they want to trade for? I guessed the next message would tell me. I wondered how they linked her to me. It must be someone who knew we were friends.

I called the station. Stosh was out at a luncheon. Rosie and Steele were out doing whatever they do when they're out. I decided to drive over and wait for someone to show up.

***

had been sitting nervously in Stosh's office for fifteen minutes when he walked in. He saw the look on my face and asked what was wrong. I repeated the message. He sat and picked up the phone.

"Marge, have you seen Steele and Lonnigan?" He sighed. "See if you can find them and get 'em in here. Spencer, did you call up north?"

"No. I came here right away."

"Okay, we'll get a tap on your line. And…"

My pager went off.

"It's the Ephraim police. I wonder how they heard about this."

"Only one way to find out." He pushed the phone over to me. I made the call and sat on the edge of the desk next to the phone. Paul answered.

"Paul, Spencer. How did you hear?"

"Hear? Hear what?"

"Hear what?" I almost yelled. "Why did you call?"

"I got a call from the Coast Guard about an hour ago."

"They found a boat?"

Paul was quiet for a long ten seconds. "No, they found a body—washed up on the rocks near Plum Island."

I was so upset about Kathleen that I hadn't caught the emotion in his voice.

I turned to Stosh. "The Coast Guard found Cletis Muddd floating up in Door."

Stosh looked surprised.

"Spencer. Spencer!"

"Yeah, Paul."

He was quiet again and I felt a chill.

"Spencer, it wasn't Muddd."

I sat down on the chair and asked without really wanting to know, "Who was it?"

"Kathleen."

I could tell by the look on Stosh's face that he knew the answer.

"Drowned? Was it an accident?"

"We'll have to wait and see. But I saw her. She was beat up pretty badly, Spencer. My guess would be she died from the beating, maybe not on purpose, and they dumped her in the water."

I sat frozen in the chair hoping that it was a bad dream. The phone was still in my hand, but my hand was in my lap.

Stosh got up and took the phone out of my hand.

"This is Lieutenant Powolski." He listened for a minute. "Do you have anything else?" He put the phone on speaker.

"No, Lieutenant. Beat up pretty bad. I'm guessing they killed her and then dumped her in the bay hoping she'd disappear. But bodies always float up somewhere. Probably someone not familiar with the waters up here. There are better places to dump a body that would take longer."

I could hear Stosh telling Paul about the kidnapping, but it was like it was happening on television. Marge came in and dropped some folders on the lieutenant's desk. She looked at me and instantly looked worried.

I felt completely disconnected from what was going on.

Stosh hung up. I could hear him talking, but it was like a dream and I was just watching. Marge looked like she floated out of the room. I could still hear Stosh talking, but it took a while before I realized he was talking to me.

"Spencer. Spencer. I'll have Lonnigan drive you home."

I had no idea why he wanted me to go home or why I couldn't drive myself. I looked at Stosh and asked a silly question. "So, if Kathleen is dead, who is my girlfriend, the one the bad guys said they're holding?" I spread my hands palms up and shook my head. "I don't even *have* a girlfriend."

Stosh buzzed Marge and asked her to come in. "Marge, please take Spencer to the break room and get some coffee while I find Lonnigan."

I shook my head, trying to get hold of something real.

"No. I'm okay. Let's talk about the girlfriend. I'm not kidding. I really *don't* have one."

Stosh sighed and squinted at me with concern. "Well, someone thinks you do. And thinking back, I could make a list as long as my arm."

"None of whom are current."

"Maybe so," he replied. "But it's how it appears to someone else. And it's that someone else who counts. Let's figure this out."

I needed to concentrate.

"Okay. I—oh crap."

"What?"

"Maxine. We just spent two days together. She was with me when I found Gunderson's body. If someone was watching the store…" I dialed the inn, feeling sick to my stomach.

Stosh told Marge he'd call her if he needed her.

Aunt Rose answered.

"Hi Aunt Rose, is…"

"Bad timing, Spencer. I'm in the middle of…"

"Rose! This is important. Is Maxine there?"

"Well, of course she is. She's upstairs making up beds."

"When was the last time you saw her?"

"Spencer." She sounded agitated. "What's this about?"

"When?"

Now she sounded worried. "I guess an hour ago. Maybe two. Why?"

"Go look. I need to know she's there."

"Okay, I'll be right back. You're scaring me."

She was back in two minutes.

"She's not in the house, Spencer. What's going on?"

"Look outside and see if you can find her. I'll hold."

That took a few minutes longer.

Out of breath, Rose said, "She's not here Spencer. What's going on?"

"Someone called me and said they had my girlfriend. She didn't tell you she was leaving?"

"No. She had some errands to do, but she usually tells me when she's leaving."

"Okay. Call Stosh when she shows up." I gave her his direct line.

"You're scaring me, Spencer. Should I call the police?"

"No. I'll call Paul. You just stay there and call as soon as she shows up." I didn't want to think she might not.

I hung up and turned back to Stosh.

"Who else could it be, Spencer?" he asked.

"My next guess is Rosie."

As Stosh pulled out a yellow legal pad, Rosie walked in.

"Marge says you want to see me."

I got up and hugged her. She looked shocked.

"Never been so happy to see you, Rosie."

Stosh's smile stretched across his face. "Me too."

"What the hell is the matter with you two?"

I explained as she sat on the chair with arms.

Steele walked in, looked at our faces, and asked who died.

Stosh filled him in.

He leaned against the door jamb and crossed his arms over his chest. "Sorry about Kathleen, Spencer. Sorry, that was the wrong thing to say."

"Don't worry about it, Steele."

"So, who's missing?" he asked.

I told him about Maxine.

The lieutenant looked up at Steele. "Where's Pitcher?"

He shrugged. "Beats me."

"Isn't she with you today?"

"She didn't show up this morning. I figured she was off with Lonnigan. I've given up trying to keep track of this screwy schedule."

I looked seriously at Stosh.

He picked up the phone and asked Marge to put out a call for Pitcher.

He hung up the phone and turned to me. "Why would anyone think she is your girlfriend?"

"No idea."

"Probably not our girl, but I'd like to find her anyway."

Rosie turned to me. "Spencer, how long were you guys together when you were waiting for me at the diner?"

"Maybe a half hour. But…"

She held up her hand. "And you said you were at the gallery before that. Could somebody have followed you?"

"I suppose. But I didn't notice anyone."

"You weren't expecting to be followed. It would have been pretty easy to do."

I hated to admit it, but she was right. "So let's say someone followed me. Why would they think she was my girlfriend?"

Rosie smiled. "When I came in you sure looked like you were with someone special. The two of you made a nice couple."

I squirmed in my chair. "That's crazy, Rosie. I just met her."

"Yes, but you have a way with women. You like them. Easy for someone to notice."

I thought about the possibility and felt awful. I hoped she was wrong.

Stosh's phone rang. He listened for ten seconds and hung up.

"Nobody has seen her. Let's assume for the moment they have Pitcher."

"Who's 'they'?" asked Steele.

"Don't know," Stosh answered.

"And what do they want?"

"Don't know that either."

I stood up. "This is about these paintings, and two are missing. I'm going back to the frame shop and take it apart. I missed something."

Stosh shook his head. "Someone already beat you to that. And *they* knew what they were looking for. You need to stay at your house and wait for a call."

"Come on, Stosh. I can't sit and do nothing. I've got to find those paintings."

"Not so easy when one of them was taken by Kathleen and she can't tell you where it is."

"Anything on *Harbor Nights*?"

Stosh wrote on his legal pad. "We've talked to the employees. Nobody knows anything."

"Who's there besides Bloom and Vitale?" I asked.

"Just one other kid—a girl who works part time. We even talked to the cleaning crew. No sign of forced entry. And before you ask, we've checked all the art channels and pawn shops—nothing."

"Maybe we should find out who bought *Green and Blue* and the others. Should be easy to find out who."

"I already did," said Rosie. "Company called Travel the World, Inc. Bloom says he has no idea who the owner is. He works through an agent."

Stosh pulled a file out of his basket. "Lawyer—Black and Reynolds."

"And you called them?"

The lieutenant looked at Rosie.

"Yes, I talked to Black. He says his client hired him so he could be anonymous. He gets paid a lot to keep it that way. I asked if he wants his stolen painting. Black said of course he does, but not at the expense of his anonymity. He assured me his client knows nothing about all of this."

"I wonder if a judge would be happy with that answer," I said.

Rosie smiled. "We may get to find out."

Nothing made any sense and no one was helping. And no one seemed concerned. The owner of the painting didn't want his name known and the gallery was owned by a hidden company with ties to organized crime. This wasn't about a painting.

"How much is *Harbor Nights* worth?" I asked.

Rosie answered. "It was insured for two grand."

"It was insured?"

"Yup. All of the paintings were insured for two grand by the gallery. They were their responsibility until they were picked up or sold."

"Maybe this is about insurance fraud," offered Stosh.

I shook my head. "If it is, I don't see how. Certainly not worth it for two grand. And Kathleen wouldn't be involved if it is. I'm thinking the two missing paintings are somehow connected."

"How?" asked Stosh.

"No clue."

"Well, when you get one, let me know."

The missing *Harbor Nights* was pretty confusing, but I had a little advantage with *Blue and Green*. I didn't know where the painting was, but I knew when Kathleen had hidden it. It must have been when she asked for extra time. I needed to have another chat with Paul.

Stosh set down his pencil. "You should get a call soon, Spencer. Go home and wait. After they call, we'll talk about what to do next." He turned to Rosie. "Lonnigan, check Pitcher's apartment and let me know. Steele, go with Spencer and get the tap set up."

As we stood up, Stosh's phone rang. He answered and just listened.

"Okay, Rose. Thanks for the call."

He turned to me. "Maxine's back. Get going Lonnigan."

"I'll go with you," I said to Rosie.

Stosh shook his head. "No you won't. You're going home to wait for a call."

I walked out with Rosie. "I feel so bad, Rosie. If they have her, it's my fault."

"Come on, Spencer. In no way is this your fault. You had no way of knowing this would happen. We'll find her."

I nodded. "The sooner the better."

She put her hand on my arm and in a soft voice said, "Spencer, I'm so sorry about Kathleen. That's horrible."

I felt the sadness starting to wash over me. "Yes, it is."

"Will you be okay?"

I put my arm around her shoulder and she circled my waist with her arm. "Sure. I just need to keep working." I didn't want to stop thinking.

"If you want some company, let me know."

I nodded. "I will, thanks."

She gave me a hug and looked up at me with caring and unspoken words.

I drove home and sat on the couch staring at the phone, trying to figure out what to do after I got the call. I figured that would depend on what the caller had to say. I could try and find *Blue and Green* and hope the Coast Guard could find Cletis. Of course, I was assuming Cletis was alive.

Chapter 24

My phone was ringing as I opened the door. It was Stosh. Pitcher wasn't home and her car was parked in front of her building. The lady across the hall had heard someone knock on her door about seven a.m., but didn't hear anything else. There was nothing in Pitcher's apartment that helped. Her purse with her police ID and badge was on her dresser.

The phone rang again at four p.m. A male voice told me he was assuming the line was tapped and the call was being traced. He assured me we wouldn't be talking that long and he asked if I was willing to make a trade.

"If I knew what I was trading, I might."

"Don't get smart, Manning. Evidently you don't care what happens to your girlfriend."

"I care a great deal." I glanced at Steele who had started the recorder. He twirled his finger in the air.

"Well, playing dumb isn't going to help her."

"I assure you I'm not playing dumb. I have no idea what you're looking for. I wish I did."

Silence.

"You'd better be on the level, Manning. Cuz if you aren't, you'll be attending your girlfriend's funeral."

"I assure you, I don't want anybody dead. But I don't know what you're talking about. Why don't you just tell me what it is you want?"

"How dumb do you think I am?"

I didn't answer that. "I want to talk to her."

He ignored me. "I'll be in touch," he said. "If you don't have better answers, I'll kill her."

He was starting to sound impatient. I wasn't sure how to respond and decided brutal honesty was best.

"Look. I'm telling you the truth. I have no idea what you want. I'm trying to find out but not having any luck. If you're not going to tell me, then you just do what you have to do."

He hung up. Steele shook his head.

"Whaddya think, P.I.?"

I moved to the couch. "I think this is nuts. What the hell does he want?"

"There's the million-dollar question."

I shrugged. "I'll tell you this—I'm not sitting around waiting for this guy to call again. I'm not going to just sit on the sidelines and wait." I had never felt so frustrated.

"I don't think the lieutenant will agree to that."

I looked him in the eye. "Don't think I'll ask."

"And when the guy calls?"

"He'll get the machine and whoever's listening will hear what he has to say. And he'll call back, just like he did this time. He doesn't want Pitcher—he wants whatever is missing. You gonna tell the lieutenant I left?"

"At some point, I'll have to. But if I go into the head and come out and you're gone that's what I'll tell him."

I nodded. "Thanks Steele. Appreciate it."

"Hey. I'm not doing it for you. I'm just covering my ass." He stood up. "Do something first. Redo your machine message. Make it twice as long and talk slow."

I did. Then I called the Ephraim police. Paul answered.

"Hey Paul, Spencer. I'd like to take another look inside Framed. Think the chief would mind?"

He laughed. "Probably. But he's in Green Bay till tomorrow afternoon. And he's at a dinner at the moment, so I can't ask."

"Is it okay with you? You could meet me there."

"I'd rather not meet you. I've got plans. How about if I leave the key at the inn in an envelope with your name on it?"

"That works. Thanks. How do you want me to get it back to you?"

"Just bring it back in the morning. But get it to me personally."

"Will do."

"And if you find anything urgent I'll be at the Greenwood."

"Right."

Steele went into the head. I picked up my bag, repacked some fresh clothes, and headed north.

Chapter 25

grabbed a fast-food burger and fries, ate in the car on the way back to Door County, and crossed the bridge in Sturgeon Bay a little after seven. A half hour later I parked in front of the cottage, dropped my bag back inside, and called Maxine. She answered the phone.

"Hi, Max. Do you know if Paul left an envelope for me?"

"He did."

"You wanna take a ride?"

"Sure. Where are we going?"

"Back to Framed. Followed by ice cream."

"Okay. I'll be on the porch."

I made it in fifteen minutes. She came down, got in the car, and handed me the envelope.

She put her hand on my arm. "I heard about your friend. I'm so sorry, Spencer."

"Thanks. This place isn't the same without her. We had our problems, but we had a lot of good times. It's so senseless." The case had taken a new turn. I was personally involved. On the drive I had thought about Kathleen and sadness had turned into anger. I vowed to get the bastard.

Ten minutes later, we parked a half block down from Framed. I didn't want some alert person writing down my license number.

"You going to wait in the car?"

"No. I think I'll take a walk." She sounded worried. "Be careful, Spencer."

"I will. Give me a head start."

There was still some light in the sky and the sidewalks were still crowded with tourists. There was a line at the frozen yogurt stand.

I let myself in and closed and locked the door. I really didn't expect to find anything and I didn't. I just wanted to be doing something. There were many times in the past when something fell out when I shook the trees.

Another look through everything took about a half hour. I was careful not to touch anything. I locked up and looked around for Maxine. I found her sitting on a bench across the street and joined her.

"Beautiful evening."

She stretched out her arms. "It definitely is."

The temperature was still in the eighties, but a north breeze had taken away the humidity.

She looked nervous. "Do you know you're being watched?"

"You mean the girl who was sitting next to you?"

"Yup."

"Well, I saw her but didn't assume she was watching me."

"Not specifically you. But she was definitely watching the store. Her name is Peggy Sue."

"I'm going to have to hire you as an operative. You get anything else?"

"No. But she's over in the yogurt line if you want to talk to her."

I picked her out of the line. "Seems like you've made a connection, Maxine. You willing to continue?"

She shrugged. "Sure, what do you have in mind?"

I handed her a five dollar bill. "Offer to buy yogurt and suggest you come back here to sit."

"Okay." She got up, started to walk away, and then turned back with a smile that melted me—just like the first one a few years back. "How much does this operative thing pay?"

"A cup of frozen yogurt."

"Well, that's a start," she said, glancing back at me over her shoulder.

I watched her talking to Peggy Sue. With short, black hair and a round face with glasses, she looked to be in her early twenties. Kinda bookish looking, except I doubted she had read any Tolstoy. Evidently Peggy Sue agreed to the suggestion because they stayed in line. Hard to beat free frozen yogurt.

They were chatting as they approached the bench. When Peggy Sue saw me she hesitated and started to tell Maxine they should sit somewhere else. Maxine stopped her.

"Peggy Sue, this is my friend, Spencer. He bought the yogurt."

She responded with a soft thanks.

"You're welcome. Please, sit." I moved to the end of the bench.

Maxine sat on the other end so Peggy Sue had to sit next to me.

"Are you visiting up here, Peggy Sue?"

Looking at the ground, she said, "No, I live here."

"Really? Where?"

"I have an apartment in Ellison Bay with my boyfriend."

I had the feeling something was going to fall out of the tree.

"Nice up there. Where is he tonight?"

She didn't answer and started eating her yogurt. Maxine had a head start.

"Did he work at Framed?"

She jumped a little and looked at me suddenly with surprise and a little fear.

"How did you know that?"

"Well, you were sitting here looking at the shop—kind of like you were waiting for someone."

She stirred her yogurt and said with a defeated look, "I don't know where he is."

"*He* would be Cletis?"

She nodded, this time without surprise. "How do you know his name?" She was looking down at the grass.

"I'm a private investigator, Peggy Sue. I've been looking into what's going on at the frame shop."

"You mean poor Mr. Gunderson?"

"Yes, there are a few things."

"Is Cletis in trouble?" She slowly lifted her spoon and took another bite and then stirred the yogurt.

"I don't know. I'd like to find him to ask some questions. When was the last time you saw him?"

"Are you going to help him?"

"I will if he hasn't done anything wrong."

She looked at me for a few seconds and her face changed from worried to relieved. She had made a decision.

Peggy Sue finished the yogurt and set the cup down next to her on the bench. "We went to Washington Island Tuesday. The ferry brought us back about five. He dropped me at the apartment and said he had some errands to do. That was the last time."

"Did he seem normal?"

"What do you mean?"

"Was he worried about anything? Did he seem nervous? Something like that."

"No. He was excited."

I glanced over at Maxine. She was listening attentively.

"Do you know what he was excited about?"

"Not exactly, but he said it wouldn't be long now."

"For what?"

"Till we were rich."

Maxine's eyebrows went up. So did my interest.

"How were you going to get rich?"

She shook her head. "I don't know. I just know that a month or so ago he said he had a plan to make us rich. He wouldn't say what it was."

"Did he say anything about paintings?" I asked hopefully.

"He didn't say anything."

"Didn't you wonder?"

"Sure, but if Cletis wants to tell you something he will. If he doesn't..." She shrugged. "...he won't."

"Why were you watching the shop?"

She looked blankly across the street. "He might come back."

I felt sorry for her. She seemed like she was lost without him. "Wouldn't it be better to wait at your apartment?"

She slowly shook her head. "I don't like to be there."

"Why not?" I asked gently.

Her eyes welled up and her bottom lip trembled. "We owe rent from last month. Cletis was going to pay yesterday when he got paid. The manager said he'd throw us out if we didn't pay up by the end of the month. That's Saturday."

"Couldn't you pay it?"

She looked embarrassed. "I don't have any money."

I felt badly for her and wanted to help. I could pay her rent but I had a better idea.

"Maxine, is the inn full?"

When she didn't answer, I looked around Peggy Sue at Maxine. There were tears in her eyes. She took a deep breath, said no, and wiped her eyes with a napkin.

"Peggy Sue, I have a place for you to stay. My aunt owns an inn in Ephraim. Maxine works there."

Looking down, she replied sadly, "I couldn't pay for that."

"You don't have to. You can have one of the empty rooms."

A family with laughing kids walked by. There was only five feet between them and Peggy Sue, but their worlds were miles apart.

"I can't take charity."

"It's not charity. Maxine is overworked. You can help out with the guests."

She looked at Maxine who nodded with a smile.

"Well, okay. That would be nice." She dabbed at her eyes with her napkin.

"Great. Let's go get your things."

"The manager isn't going to be happy."

"Don't worry. I'll take care of him."

Maxine patted her shoulder.

We drove up to Ellison Bay and Maxine helped Peggy Sue pack. I emptied Cletis' drawers into a suitcase. On the third trip to the car, a short, mean-looking man walked over from the office. If he was looking for trouble, it was his lucky day.

"What's going on here?" he asked warily.

"Peggy Sue is moving out."

"Not without paying, she's not."

"Well, technically, you gave her till the end of the month. So she can do whatever she wants till then. And you were going to throw her out anyway so she's just saving you the trouble."

"She owes me two months' rent and I want my money," he said with a sneer.

"You'll get it." What he *deserved* to get was a kick in the teeth.

"Are you telling me by the end of the month she's going to pay two months' rent?"

"No. She doesn't have any money. But if you'll wait till tomorrow, I'll stop back and write you a check. How much is it?"

"Who the hell are you?" he spat.

I took two steps forward and looked down at him. "The guy signing the check. How much?"

"One seventy-five a month. She owes for two."

"Fine." I turned and walked back to the apartment, hoping he would make one more comment. I had run out of patience. Maxine and Peggy Sue were just coming out with their arms full.

"What did *he* say?" asked Peggy Sue with concern.

I took the suitcase and put it in the trunk. "Don't worry about him. Is there more?"

"One more trip," said Maxine. "There are a couple bags of food."

On the drive back, Peggy Sue asked how Cletis would find her. I told her I left word with the manager. She didn't need to know I'd tell him myself when I found him.

As we drove, I asked if Cletis cared about her.

"What do you mean?"

"Does he care about you? Would he worry about you, wonder if you were okay? Would he run off and leave you alone?"

She looked like she was going to cry.

"Sure he does. Why are you asking that?"

"How long have you known each other?"

She tried to stop a trembling lip by biting on it. "Since fifth grade. We went to school together in Tennessee."

"And how did you end up here?"

"He got into some trouble. It was better that he left. A friend of his had a friend in Chicago who said he could get him a job. Why are you asking all that?"

"Just wondering, Peggy Sue. Just wondering if he cares about you."

I made a mental list of the fruit that was falling out of the tree.

It was dark by the time we got back to the inn. I went in first to explain the situation to Aunt Rose.

She was just coming down the stairs when I walked in. She hurried over and put her arms around me. When she pulled away there were tears in her eyes.

"Oh, Spencer, this is so sad. Thanks for calling me and letting me know. I just can't believe anyone would do that to such a sweet person."

I kept my arm around her. "There are people who would do that to anybody, Aunt Rose. I have something I want to talk to you about."

I told her about Peggy Sue and that I would pay for the room. I asked if she would find some work for her to do. She was glad to and told me I didn't have to pay.

The three of us brought in Peggy Sue's things and Rose showed her to her room. I sat in a rocker on the porch and waited for Maxine. Lights danced out in the harbor.

The screen door squeaked open ten minutes later. Maxine came over and gave me a kiss on the forehead.

"What's that for?"

"For being wonderful. And if it weren't for you, I'd still be…"

I patted her arm. "Not as wonderful as you think. It's more selfish. She might lead Cletis here. It's more than I had three hours ago."

"Whatever you say." She sat in the rocker next to me. "Why *did* you ask that?"

"Ask what?"

"If he cared about her."

"I wanted to know how much leverage I have."

She stopped rocking. "Leverage?"

Coming out of her mouth it didn't sound so pretty.

"Leverage. If he doesn't care about her, I have none. If he does, the fact that I helped his girlfriend will hopefully make him more cooperative, if he ever shows up."

She looked like she was thinking, and I wasn't happy about what I thought she was thinking.

"So, kinda like they have your girlfriend, so you have his?"

"At the risk of cracking the pedestal you have me up on—kinda. But I have a feeling Pitcher isn't being so well taken care of. And Peggy Sue is free to go any time she wants. Just leverage, not kidnapping."

Her eyes twinkled above a little smirk. "The pedestal is still intact. Your offer was made out of a kind heart. As time went by, you saw how it might help with the Cletis situation. I can't blame you for being good at your job."

I looked at her and squinted. This wasn't the first time Maxine had shown a flare for good intuition and common sense.

A family with two kids walked up the stairs and said hello. We sat there in silence for an hour watching the running lights on boats returning to harbor.

Chapter 26

I made pancakes for breakfast and headed for Ephraim as the sun was just peeking over the tree tops. It was going to be another hot day. I parked in front of the police station on Highway 42. Paul was making coffee.

"Want a cup?"

"Sure." I sat down on one of the two chairs next to his desk and threw the envelope with the key inside on the top.

He put a mug of coffee down in front of me and sat on the chair next to mine. "Find anything?"

"Not inside." I told him about Peggy Sue.

"Interesting. You think she knows something she's not sharing?"

I took a sip. It was too hot for a drink. "Nope. She has no clue. And she's worried. If she knew where he was, she wouldn't be."

"What's your guess on the getting rich part?"

The phone rang. He picked it up on the first ring and told someone the chief would be back later in the afternoon.

I blew on the coffee. "Your guess is as good as mine. Drugs?"

He rolled a pencil between two fingers. "What would drugs have to do with paintings? How about stolen paintings?"

I shook my head. "We're talking paintings by Kathleen. Not worth that much."

He agreed. "How about insurance?"

"Nope. They were insured for two thousand. Not much there."

He took a drink and pushed the mug back and forth by the handle. "Well, this whole gallery setup doesn't make sense. How about she painted over a valuable painting?"

"You're watching too much television." I blew on my coffee and took another sip.

"It's possible."

"Not very. Kathleen would have to be in on it and there's no way. She was a little crazy, but there wasn't a dishonest bone in her body."

"Yeah, I guess."

"You think the Coast Guard is still looking?"

"Yup. They'll keep the bulletins live till we cancel them. They have to show up sooner or later. Not easy to hide a boat."

"Sooner would be better. We've got a kidnapped detective."

"Yeah, strange."

I told him about Larry Maggio.

He whistled. "That adds another level to this. Must be something huge if those guys are involved. But why would Cletis think he was going to get rich?"

"How about he saw a way to steal from the big boys and then figured on disappearing."

"Pretty dangerous."

"Yeah, but I have a feeling Cletis isn't too bright. And maybe he didn't know who he was stealing from. I only found out about Maggio because someone did some serious digging."

He took a drink and turned the handle away from him. "So, the mob has something going on. Cletis somehow gets wind of it and wants to cut himself in. But he doesn't know about the mob."

"Which brings us back to paintings. That's how Cletis got involved." I took another drink. "You have any idea what Kathleen did when you gave her time to turn herself in?"

"I'm guessing she hid the painting."

"Well, yeah. I was more wondering where. No idea where she went?"

"Nope. You want some more coffee?"

"No thanks. I'm going to hit the road for home."

"Aren't you getting tired of making that trip?"

I laughed. "I just point the car and it finds the way by itself."

Paul stood up and took the mugs to the counter. "When are you coming back?"

"No clue. Depends on what happens."

"Okay. I'll let you know if we get anything."

"Thanks, Paul. Appreciate it."

I stopped for gas in Sturgeon Bay. The thermometer at the station read 92. Pretty hot for the end of June. And the weather man was saying it was going to get hotter. Something about a stalled system over the Midwest. I decided I needed to spend more time on the deck at the cottage where the bay kept temperatures down a few degrees.

Chapter 27

As I passed the turnoff to Sheboygan my pager vibrated. It was Lieutenant Powolski. This would not be good. I decided to wait until I got home for my tongue lashing.

I pulled into my drive about one o'clock. There wasn't a cloud in the sky and the heat in Chicago was worse than Door. Steele's car was in front. This time I brought my bag into the bedroom, hoping I'd get to unpack it. Steele was watching the Lead Off Man show before the Friday Cubs game, the first of the weekend series with the Cardinals. There was a commercial running for Danley Garages.

"Hi P.I. Short vacation."

"Some vacation. I got paged by the lieutenant. He knows?"

"Oh yeah."

"What'd he say?"

Steele shrugged. "Said he wasn't surprised."

"Hmmm. I'll bet he'll have thought of more by now. No calls?"

"No calls. This whole damned thing is pretty strange. I get the feeling whoever this is doesn't know what the hell he's doing."

"I agree. Nothing about this is professional. The two killings were pretty sloppy. If you want somebody to talk, you don't beat them so badly that you kill them. And when I told the guy I had no idea what he was talking about, he didn't know what to do."

Steele nodded. "You gonna call the lieutenant?"

"I suppose I'd better face the music."

I called. Marge answered and said he had just walked down the hall. She asked me to hold. He came on the line two minutes later.

"Spencer. Nice of you to bless us with your presence."

"Look, Stosh…"

"I'll lecture you later. The Coast Guard found the boat with your boy Cletis aboard."

"Where? When?"

"About two hours ago a boat from Station Wilmette spotted the boat heading south about two miles offshore of Belmont harbor. They boarded it and detained Cletis on a stolen boat charge. Lonnigan and Parker are bringing him back here."

"They find anything on the boat?"

"Don't know. We'll know more when they get back."

"Okay. I'm coming in."

"No, you're not. Stay put in case these morons call. We'll fill you in later."

"Okay." I hung up and told Steele about the boat.

"Progress."

"I hope so."

We watched the Cubs and Cards for two hours. By the end of the seventh it was six to two Cubs. The phone rang in the middle of the eighth inning. Steele slipped on the headset, started the recorder, and pointed at me.

"Manning."

"Spencer, it's Rosie."

Steel took off the headset and stopped the recorder.

"Hey, Rosie."

"Hi. You okay?"

"The thinking part is fine. You get anything from Cletis?"

"Not much. But we don't want to tie up the line. I'm coming over. You want anything to eat?"

"That would be great." I put my hand over the receiver. "Steele, you have lunch?"

He shook his head.

"Neither of us had any lunch. Why don't you pick up a bag of burgers."

"Will do. See you in a half."

While we waited for Rosie, we watched the Cubs try to give the game away. When the doorbell rang it was six to five, Cubs, in the top of the ninth and the Cards had the bases loaded with one out.

***

I turned on the TV in the kitchen and Rosie spread the burgers and fries out on the table. I had a Schlitz. They had Cokes. I gave Rosie a ten for the food and got the ketchup.

The Cubs switched pitchers and brought in Clint Coleman. I just shook my head as I unwrapped a cheeseburger. Were they *trying* to lose the game? The guy had an E.R.A. of seven. He did strike out two batters, but gave up a walk in between to tie the game.

As I took a bite, I asked Rosie, "So, what do we got?"

"Not much besides the stolen boat, and even that's iffy since they knew each other. He says Gunderson told him he could use it whenever he wanted."

"How about the murder?"

"He started out looking surprised to hear about it, then admitted that he found Gunderson dead on the floor." She dipped a fry in ketchup.

"And just left him there?"

"I guess. Says he was scared. Whoever did it might be after him, too. So he ran."

"After him for what?" I took a long drink.

"Good question. He had no answer—just after him."

"You ask about the missing paintings?"

"He says he knows nothing about it."

I took another bite. Steele's was gone already.

Jim Hickman led off the Cubs half of the ninth with a home run and Clint Coleman was off the hook.

"Did he mention anything about a girlfriend?"

"Girlfriend?"

"Yeah, seems he left her behind to be thrown out of their apartment tomorrow."

"Nice guy. Nope, nothing."

Didn't sound like much caring there. I might have to rethink my leverage.

"Did you ask why he was going to Chicago?"

She nodded while chewing.

"Let me guess. No answer."

She managed to get out a muffled *right*.

Steele gathered the trash and tossed it in the garbage can.

"Can I have a chat with him?"

"Okay with me. I'll run it by the lieutenant. What makes you think you can get somewhere?"

"Leverage." I told her more about the girlfriend. Steele went back to the living room.

Rosie got the okay and I followed her back to the station.

Chapter 28

The desk sergeant said Lieutenant Powolski wanted to see me before I did anything else. I asked if that included breathing and got a dirty look.

I knocked on the door frame, walked in, and sat down.

"You miss me?"

"Yeah, like I miss hemorrhoids." He finished making notes, put a piece of paper back in a folder and filed it in the drawer behind him.

"I looked into Chief Iverson. I thought the name sounded familiar. He started his career as a beat cop in Chicago twenty years ago. Guess who his partner was?"

"Now how the hell would I know that?"

"Would I ask if you couldn't make an educated guess?"

"No?"

"No. So…"

"Uh, you?"

"You're an idiot. If he was my partner, don't you think I'd remember that a little more clearly?"

"I guess. This isn't a fun game. I give up."

He looked like he wanted to throw something at me. "Steele."

That was a surprise. "Really? Interesting. We'll have to have a chat."

"He took a detective job in Milwaukee after five years on the street and took the chief job a few years ago."

"What's his record?"

"Nothing outstanding, but not negative. Did his job. Didn't piss anyone off."

"Till he met me."

"I can't hold that against him. What is it you want to ask Muddd?"

I ran my hands down the smooth arms of the chair and told him about the girlfriend. "I figure he knows something about the paintings. He's the one who took *Blue and Green* in the first place. I'd like to know why. And he might know what our kidnapper is looking for. And I'd like to know if he knows about Mr. Maggio."

"And you think he'll answer all those questions?"

I told Stosh about the girlfriend angle. "I'm hoping he'll open up when I tell him about Peggy Sue."

Stosh folded his arms. "Give it a shot. I'll have him brought to interview two. Lonnigan will be watching."

"You arresting him?"

"I need someone to press charges for stealing the boat and the owner is dead. Doesn't seem worth pursuing. Door County Sheriff wants to talk to him about the Gunderson murder. By the way, the medical examiner puts the time of death between three and five. Also, there was no water in Kathleen's lungs. She was dead when they dumped her in the water."

I nodded. "Thanks. Muddd ask for a lawyer?"

"He refused. Doesn't seem too smart."

"Maybe he thinks the truth will set him free."

"Yeah, good luck with that."

***

Cletis was sitting at a wooden desk when I walked in. A female officer left the room. He looked tired and scared. He wasn't exactly as I pictured him, but close. Not taller than five foot six, sandy brown hair that not only wasn't combed but probably would refuse the effort, blue eyes a little too far apart, and a small mouth with almost no lips. I wondered what Peggy Sue saw in him. His eyes darted around the room, sometimes stopping on me.

"Cletis, I'm Spencer Manning. I'm a private investigator. I'd like to ask you a few questions."

"They already asked me questions," he said with too much bravado for the guy sitting on the wrong side of the table.

"Yes, they did. There are two people dead. One is…"

"Two? I only know one."

"One is Gunderson. You said you walked in and found him on the floor. Right?"

"Yes," he answered meekly. The bravado was gone. Evidently, thinking about Gunderson had an effect.

"What time was that?"

"About six."

"Was the door locked when you got there?"

"Yes." He tapped the table with his right forefinger.

"Why did you go there then?"

He squirmed in the chair and kneaded his hands. "Do I have to answer your questions? You're not a cop."

"No, you don't."

"Then why should I?"

I managed to make eye contact. "Because I don't think you're involved in the murders. And if you're involved in anything else, and you cooperate, they'll go easy on you."

He didn't respond.

"And because Peggy Sue cares about you."

His eyes widened and his mouth opened and closed. "How do you know about Peggy Sue?"

"I met her in Fish Creek and found her a place to stay."

He bowed his head into his hands. "Where is she staying? She doesn't have any money."

"At my friend's inn in Ephraim. She's working there for room and board."

"She's okay?"

"She's fine. Why did you come to Chicago?"

He looked nervous again and clenched his left fist.

"I needed money. Gunderson was supposed to pay me Wednesday but…"

"How were you going to get money here?"

He looked right at me but didn't answer.

"Okay. Why did you take the boat? Why didn't you just drive?"

"I wanted to leave the car for Peggy Sue."

"How did you get the key for the boat?"

"I had a key to his house. He sent me there a lot to pick up things. The boat key was on a hook. Gunderson let me and Peggy Sue go for rides if he wasn't using it. I wasn't stealing it, just borrowing it—honest."

"Let's talk about the store. I found him and called the police. When I got there the door was unlocked. Did you lock it when you left?"

"I don't know. Maybe not. I just wanted to get out of there." He looked up at me. "Who else is dead?"

"Kathleen Johnson."

The look on his face was shock. "Kathleen? Kathleen is dead?"

"Murdered. She was beaten to death."

"Oh, damn." He shook his head. "She was a nice lady. She gave us things for our apartment."

"Cletis. Both of them were beaten, like someone was trying to get them to tell something. Do you have any idea what that might be?"

He shifted in the chair and his eyes started to dart again. I had the feeling that he knew.

"No. How would I know?"

"There's also been a kidnapping. I got a call offering to trade the person kidnapped for something the caller thought I had."

"So?"

"So, I have no idea what they want to trade for. Do you?"

He didn't answer.

"Cletis, I think both answers are the same. And if you do know something about it, you're going to prison as an accessory to murder and kidnapping even if you didn't do those."

"How do I know they won't blame me for those anyway? Cops don't like me."

"Because I believe you didn't do them. You are involved in something, but it's not murder or kidnapping. I already took care of Peggy Sue. I'd like you two to get together again."

"Can I talk to her?"

"I'll see. One more question. There were duck decoys in the store. Who was doing the carving?"

"Gunderson. He was a genius with wood. He could make a piece of wood come alive."

"Okay. Thanks."

I got up and knocked on the door and the officer opened it. We switched places.

Rosie met me in the hall.

"So, can we set up the call?"

"How is that going to help?"

"My leverage. I think if he sees I took care of her he'll trust me."

"Wait here." She walked toward Stosh's office.

***

Rosie was back in ten minutes with a phone.

"Plug it in and get her on speaker so you and I can hear."

The officer and I changed places again.

"Okay, Cletis. I'm going to call the inn and get Peggy Sue on the line. I'll put her on the speaker so I can hear."

He looked suspicious. "And I get to talk to her?"

"You do. Ask her anything you want. Okay?"

He nodded hesitantly.

Maxine answered the phone. I explained that I had found Cletis and he wanted to talk to Peggy Sue. She went to get her.

I pushed the speaker button. A minute later Peggy Sue came on.

"Cletis? Cletis, are you there?" She sounded almost frantic.

"Hi, Peggy Sue. Are you okay?"

"Yes, thanks to these nice people. You won't believe what happened."

"Where are you?"

"You know that inn, the Harbor Lantern, in Ephraim just down the street from Wilson's Ice Cream?"

"Yeah."

"Well, that's where. I met Maxine and Mr. Manning and he got me a job there so I'd have a place to stay. There's this nicest lady, Rose, who makes the best breakfasts."

He still looked suspicious. "And what do you have to do for all this?"

"Just work. You know, make beds, wash dishes, and…"

"Peggy Sue. What about the manager? We owe him money."

"I don't know, Cletis. Mr. Manning said not to worry about him. Cletis, where are you?"

"I'm in Chicago."

"Why didn't you tell me where you were going? Why are you in Chicago?"

He twisted the cord around his finger. "I'm sorry, Peggy Sue. I came to get money. There's this guy who owes me some."

"Okay. Did you get it?"

"Well, not exactly."

"That's okay. You can live here, too. And I have a job to pay for it. We can be happy, like we talked about in Tennessee. When are you coming back?"

"I'm not sure. Soon. I have some business to take care of."

"Okay. But please hurry."

"Sure thing, Peggy Sue. Goodbye."

"Bye, Cletis."

He untwisted the cord and hung up. He looked down at the table and played with the cord for several minutes before he spoke.

"Why did you do all that for her?"

"Because she needed help. So do you, Cletis."

"What did she mean, you said not to worry about the manager?"

"I paid your rent. Peggy Sue will pay me back. You can pay me back."

He tossed the cord at the phone. "Not if I'm in jail."

"I can't help if you don't talk to me." I tried to sound reassuring.

His eyes darted around the room and then settled on the table. "There were some things I was doing."

I looked at him and asked myself if I would be talking like he was about to. The answer was no. I would have asked for a lawyer a long time ago.

"Cletis, excuse me for a few minutes. I'll be right back."

He just looked at me like he didn't have a choice.

I switched with the officer again and let myself into the room where Rosie was watching.

"You're doing great, Spencer. You were sure right about the phone call."

"Yeah, well, I don't feel so good about being right. He needs a lawyer."

"He already refused."

I nodded. "Yes, he did. And I sure want to hear what he has to say. But I'm pretty sure I just talked him into a jail cell."

"We can make him state's witness and grant him immunity."

"Well, *we* can't. But it could be done—depending on what he's involved in. I'm not going to take a chance on what he has to say landing him in jail."

"Those damn morals."

"There *is* a way."

She cocked her head and raised a hand, palm up. "And that is?"

"Ben."

"Ben. Call him."

I did. And then I called home—still no calls from the kidnapper.

Chapter 29

According to Ben, he was now leading the good life without responsibilities or a committed relationship. But there were a few times I had convinced him to put on a suit. After a brief explanation about the Cletis situation, he said he'd take on Cletis as a client, listen to what he had to say, and give me an opinion about the guy's exposure. I took him out for a few beers Friday night.

We got the required Cubs talk out of the way. As usual, they looked good on paper but not so good on the field. We switched to Cletis over the second round.

"Run the confused paintings by me again." He tossed a handful of peanuts into his mouth. "I'm confused." He smiled.

I made patterns in the sweat on the side of the bottle with my finger. "Understandable. Join the club. Kathleen had a favorite painting, *Blue and Green*. The gallery in Chicago had been trying to buy it, but she wouldn't sell. The frame shop in Fish Creek acts as an intermediary between Kathleen and the Simmons Gallery in Chicago. They pick up…"

"Why didn't she deal directly with the gallery?"

"I was going to ask her that, but…" I took a drink. "I did ask her brother. All he could say was that's how her father did it."

"And why did her father do it?"

I glared at him.

He looked amused. "You're no fun to play with. So when her father died, they made the same deal with Kathleen?"

"Yup."

"She inherited her father's talent?"

"Hardly. I've been thinking about that. I'm thinking they didn't care about the paintings, but about the process."

"Meaning?"

"Meaning both her father and Kathleen provided something someone needed. It was just an added benefit that her father's work was good."

"And what was it they needed?"

I shook my head and finished the second beer. "Don't know. And the two people who might know are dead."

Ben took a drink and swirled what was left in the bottom. "You're hoping another person might be Cletis."

"Yup. He says he was involved in something."

"So what about the confusion?"

"The gallery made out a list of paintings they wanted. On that list was a painting called *Green and Blue*. The frame shop would get the paintings on the list, frame them, and ship them to Chicago. Cletis picked up thirteen paintings two Saturdays ago when Kathleen wasn't there and grabbed a wrong painting, *Blue and Green*. But a *Green and Blue* was the one on the list. I asked Gunderson about it and he said he just figured the kid had made a mistake and was confused by the similar names. But both *Green and Blue* and *Blue and Green* were gone."

"Did Gunderson check the paintings before they were shipped?"

"No. Cletis did all the framing. Gunderson had no reason to think the paintings were wrong."

"Okay. So just an honest mistake."

"Seems so. But Kathleen wanted her favorite painting back. Knowing Kathleen, she thought the gallery was trying to steal it from her. The employee at Simmons, Tony, says he saw her walking out with a painting on Wednesday. He says it was *Harbor Nights*. But when the curator of the gallery took an inventory of what was shipped, all thirteen were there. And *Blue and Green* wasn't on the manifest."

Ben looked confused. I couldn't blame him. "So, if all thirteen were there... what did she take?"

I shrugged. "Vitale and Bloom are sticking to their story of Kathleen taking *Harbor Nights*. But we just have Vitale's word that she even took anything, much less what it was. And Bloom didn't see anything. Maybe Cletis was confused and made an honest mistake and fourteen paintings were sent to Chicago. Kathleen took her painting and that left the correct amount of thirteen."

"Sounds plausible. So why did Lonnigan and Steele go after her?"

"Because when the gallery started to display the paintings the next day, one *was* missing—*Harbor Nights*. The curator assumed that was what was taken by Kathleen."

"But they counted thirteen the day before."

"Yes. Curious. Bloom said they miscounted. All he knew was there was a missing painting."

"Had he checked the names against the shipping list the day before?"

"No. Just counted them."

"I need another beer."

I caught the bartender's attention and held up two fingers.

Ben asked, "Both paintings are still missing?"

I nodded.

"Does Door County want Cletis for the murder?"

"Well, they want to question him. They're sending someone to get him tomorrow. But he's got a good alibi."

"Sure. I've heard that before."

"His'll be checked, but it's good. He and his girlfriend, Peggy Sue, took the car to Washington Island for the day. The ferry got them back at five. Time of death is between three and five."

Ben tilted the bottle up and grabbed some more peanuts. "Something's bothering me. If he was killed then, why were you the one to find him, especially with the door unlocked? Lotsa people up there in the summer. Why didn't a customer find the body?"

"Tourists aren't his customers. Gunderson did framing for clients And the shop is at the outer edge of the shopping district. Most people don't get down that far." I thought about the door. "Here's what I think happened. Whoever killed Gunderson walked in while the shop was open and then locked the door on the way out. Then Cletis unlocked the door, let himself in, found Gunderson, and left in a hurry without locking the door which was unlocked when I got there."

Ben rubbed the back of his neck. "This is giving me a headache, but that does explain it. Well, sounds to me like Cletis is in the clear. No one is going to pursue the boat charge and he has an alibi for the murder—at least that one."

I looked up at him. "And it might just be a matter of time before they ask him about the other one. Kathleen was probably put in the water from a boat and Cletis had a boat. But I'm guessing the same person is responsible for both, and Cletis didn't kill Gunderson."

"Makes sense. Okay, I could use a break. I'll run up to Door tomorrow and take care of Cletis. I don't see them holding him. If all goes well, you can have a chat with him."

I raised my glass in Ben's direction and then finished what was left.

"Think you can find me a room?" he asked with a smile.

"I'll make a call."

Chapter 30

Lieutenant Powolski requested that I spend the weekend at home in case there was a call. He offered to come over Saturday afternoon and play gin and watch the Cubs. This time I complied. Steele showed up at one and told me he had the afternoon shift. I warned him about Stosh's visit. He was less than thrilled. I let him get settled before I asked him about Iverson.

"I hear you spent some time with Iverson."

A wistful look faded quickly. "We were beat cops a long time ago. I hear he made it to the top."

"I guess, if you consider a two-man force that has to hand things off to the sheriff the top."

"Well, there is that *chief* in front of his name."

I got out the cards and set up the card table. "He wasn't too friendly."

"I'm not surprised," he said with a wide grin.

"Why?"

"There was an incident. He was pretty much thrown under the bus to save some brass ass. Completely screwed. He had to bend over and take it and he wasn't happy. When he got the chance to move up the ladder it was in Milwaukee. He was happy to leave."

"So a small town is perfect."

"Yup."

I chuckled. "I bet he got a big kick out of you guys losing a prisoner."

He smiled. "I bet he did."

"You have lunch?"

"I did. But I could still be hungry."

"Okay, I'll scare up some sandwiches." I walked toward the kitchen.

"Hey, P.I."

"Yeah?"

"That incident with Iverson? The brass backed up a P.I. who was a friend of the captain. They took his word instead of Iverson's."

Nice.

Lieutenant Powolski showed up at a quarter to two, put a six pack of Schlitz in the fridge, and then briefed me on what to say if the kidnapper called.

The phone rang a few minutes later. Steele got ready and pointed. It was Ben.

***

Hey, Spencer. The county sheriff is holding Cletis till Monday when the sheriff gets back from a seminar in Milwaukee. Cletis can't make bail—$20,000. You want to post it?"

"No. Won't hurt him to sit for a couple days. And he's safe in there. You talk to him?"

"Yes. Same story. I told him I thought he wouldn't be charged if the alibi checks out. Ephraim police are checking the ferry records."

"That would be Paul—a cousin of Kathleen. Have you met him?"

"No. Maybe I'll stop by there Monday."

"Did you ask Cletis about what he was involved in?"

"No. All I want to know about is what's pertinent to these two cases. I'll leave that to you once he's released."

"Okay. How's the room?"

"Wonderful. Cherry pie baking as we speak."

"I'll dream about it."

"When are you coming?"

"I'll leave Monday morning if all goes well."

"Okay. Let's meet here. Hopefully Cletis will be out by then. Hey. Do you know his last name has three Ds?"

"Yup. Unique."

"Odd. See ya."

I hung up and brought two beers to the card table. I was tired of explaining Cletis' name. The Cubs and Cards were in the second with no score. The phone rang again a half hour later. Steele got ready.

"Hello."

"Manning?"

"Yup. Who's this?"

"I ask the questions. Have you decided to be helpful yet?"

Stosh watched with apprehension.

"I don't do anything till I know the girl is okay."

"She is."

"Pardon me if I don't take your word for that. I want to talk to her."

"She's not here."

"Where is she?" It was worth a shot.

"Not here, big shot."

"Well, then we're at an impasse."

"A what?"

I sighed. "I evidently have something you want. But if I can't talk to her, I'm not talking."

He was silent for a few seconds. I looked at Steele. He looked hopeful.

"Be there at eight tonight." And he hung up.

"Shit!" said Steele. He took off the headset and banged it on the table. "Just a few more seconds."

Stosh was dealing the cards. "I think it's a pretty good assumption that the murders and the kidnapping are the same guy. Pretty sloppy. This isn't someone who knows what he's doing."

I agreed. "Not good for Pitcher. He's already killed twice."

"Yeah, but probably by mistake. Killing them didn't get him anything. If it had, he wouldn't have taken Pitcher."

"Had any luck following up on her?"

He spread his cards. "Not much. The guy who knocked on the door evidently had a good enough story to get her to open the door. Her purse, with her badge inside, was left on her dresser. The purse wasn't open so maybe the guy doesn't know she's a cop."

"Nothing from the neighbor?"

"Nope."

"Maybe another trip to Simmons," I suggested.

"We've been there several times. Either they know nothing or they're good at playing dumb." He finished his beer. "I think the key is up in Door. That's where the murders have occurred and places have been trashed."

I picked a card. "You staying?"

"Yup. We'll order some pizza for dinner. Gin." He was ahead by a buck eighty.

***

The closer it got to eight, the more nervous I got, and the grumpier Stosh got. The phone didn't ring at eight. And it hadn't rung by ten when Stosh left and Steele's relief showed up. I talked him into a game of gin and won back my buck eighty.

Chapter 31

Every policeman in the city and the suburbs was keeping a lookout for Pitcher and they had nothing. Two problems with amateurs—they were dangerous and they weren't predictable. Stosh was concerned because they hadn't called. I figured they just didn't know what to do or were arguing about what to do. That could be good and it could be bad. As long as they thought I had what they wanted, Pitcher would be safe.

The forecast for Monday was temperatures in the nineties and afternoon storms as the ground heated up. I hoped it would be cooler up in Door.

I packed a bag, said goodbye to the detective, and backed out of the garage. I slowed as I noticed a car parked across the driveway. It was a black Ford with tinted windows. I stopped just before the sidewalk and got out of the car. The passenger door opened, and a big guy got out who looked like he was used to getting his way and didn't care what anyone thought about it. A black suit fit perfectly over a barrel chest that sported a thin, black tie.

"You Manning?"

"Do I have a choice?"

He opened the rear door of the sedan. "Mister Maggio would like to have a chat with you."

"I can't think of a better way to start the week, but I've got other plans."

He didn't react.

I started to get back in the car, hoping that the detective in the house would notice what was going on. But he was in the dining room with no view of the street.

The big guy took a few steps toward me. "Perhaps I wasn't clear. There aren't any options." On a face that looked like it had been chiseled out of granite, the only thing that moved were his lips.

"There are always options."

"My mistake. Of course there are. We can do this the easy way or the hard way. This is the easy way."

I *did* prefer the easy way, and I reasoned that if they were willing to grab me in broad daylight on the street I probably wasn't in any danger. And maybe I'd pick up a piece or two of the puzzle.

"I need to turn off the car."

He nodded toward the back seat. "You get in. I'll turn off the car." He did and handed me the keys.

The driver headed east and took Lake Shore Drive south.

***

No one spoke while we were driving. I watched sailboats out on the lake, all colors of the rainbow cutting through the choppy water. We stopped in front of an office building on Michigan Avenue. The big guy opened the door for me and accompanied me in the elevator up to the thirty-second floor. The elevator opened into a hallway with one office across the hall. There was no name on the door. A lot of floor-to-ceiling glass showed a large suite with a receptionist just inside the door and two men in dark suits sitting to the left of her desk reading newspapers. They were both smoking and sharing an ashtray on a table between them. My escort motioned me to a seat and disappeared through a door in a frosted glass wall. The girl at the desk smiled and showed off her dimples. Windows showed a view of other office buildings.

A few minutes passed before the big guy reappeared and beckoned to me with his forefinger. Not much of a talker. I followed through the open door. The big guy closed the door and stayed outside.

Behind the frosted glass was a large, bright space with a glass and aluminum desk off to one side. It was bright because all the windows were floor-to-ceiling glass just like the reception area. Seated at the desk was an immaculate, thirties-looking man who looked me over while I looked over the office. He wore a perfectly tailored gray suit with a powder-blue handkerchief in the breast pocket that matched his tie. His nails were manicured and not a hair was out of place.

The view out over the lake and the harbor was an improvement over the reception area. I hoped he let his receptionist come in once in a while to see what management got to look at. From the looks of her, I had a feeling he did.

He motioned me to a chair and said tersely, "Please have a seat, Mr. Manning."

I sat in a white leather chair that would have accommodated Nero Wolfe. I looked at him and waited.

He stood up and moved to a glass-topped credenza with open glass shelves above that matched his desk. On the shelves was an excellently stocked bar. He pulled down a bottle of Macallan 18 scotch and poured an inch into each of two glasses. He put down the bottle, picked up the glasses, and handed one to me. I took it and set it down on the desk.

"You're not going to drink with me?"

He should have felt insulted, but just looked curious.

"We haven't even been introduced."

He smiled as he sat down. "My apologies. I am Larry Maggio. You are Spencer Manning, private investigator, cop's son, out to make a name for yourself."

If he was trying to win me over, he wasn't succeeding. I stared at him as he sipped the whiskey.

"Finest single-malt whiskey there is." He nodded at my glass. "I don't like to drink alone."

"And I don't like being kidnapped." I could be belligerent, too.

Another smile appeared slowly as he turned the glass in his hands. "I beg to differ. I don't see any ropes. You weren't hit over the head. I don't see anyone standing over your chair, and you have a glass of fine whiskey sitting in front of you. Many men would trade places with you in a second."

"There's no bump on my head, but there was a veiled threat. I'm not stupid."

"No, you're not."

"So why am I here?" I glanced at the glass.

He took a deep breath. "Right down to business. I like that." He took another sip and looked out the window. "Beautiful view. I spend a lot of time looking out at the lake and thinking. Lately, I've been thinking about you. You seem to be showing up everywhere I've got trouble. So I figure maybe you're part of the trouble."

I rearranged myself in the chair. "Maybe the trouble was there before I got there." I was tired of pointing that out.

He was still looking out the window, thinking. I had the feeling that no amount of thinking on his part would do any good.

"Maybe it was. But something of mine is missing. Any ideas about that?"

"That's an interesting choice of words on both accounts." I picked up the glass but didn't drink. The scotch had a rich, golden-amber color. "You're not the first to use them."

That got his interest. He looked back at me with slightly narrowed eyes.

"A friend of mine has been kidnapped. They tell me they'll trade for what I have of theirs. Maybe you have something to do with the calls."

I watched his face. It didn't change.

"Kidnapping isn't my style, Manning."

I looked at him with a slight smile and raised eyebrows.

He smiled, almost imperceptibly. "I told you, you are my guest."

"Sure. Well, I told the caller the same thing I'm telling you—I have no idea what you're talking about. And I had a police chief also tell me he found trouble everywhere I showed up. I gave him the same answer I just gave you."

He was looking out the window again.

I continued. "I do wish I knew what was going on, because a woman's life is at stake."

As he finished the whiskey, he said, "As I already said, I am not aware of any kidnapping."

My eyebrows went up. "Hmmm. Are you aware of two murders? One of those was a friend of mine."

He looked directly at me. "For not knowing anything, you have a lot of information."

"Perhaps we can swap. What is it you're missing?"

"Well, that's a little delicate. If you had it you wouldn't be asking."

"Ah yes, delicate. Meaning not quite aboveboard, I assume. So you're not going to swap?"

"No. But I would like to know more about your information."

"Okay. There's a gallery, Simmons, on Clark Street. Know of it?"

He slowly shook his head.

"That's surprising. You own it."

"I do? And where do you get your information?"

"A little bird. Perhaps MaxAMillion rings a bell."

The bell rang. "Ah, that explains it. My holding company. I own hundreds of companies, Mr. Manning. I'd be lucky to name five of them."

"Yeah, it's tough being rich."

He looked out the window again. "So what about this Simmons Gallery?"

"They have a relationship with a frame shop up in Door County. This all started with a couple of stolen paintings. Then the owner of the frame shop was killed, followed by an artist whose paintings are currently being shown at the gallery."

"That is unfortunate." He looked back to me. "And you are implying I had something to do with that? I assure you, I am an honest businessman. My money comes from commerce. I support more charities than you have heard of. I even get Christmas cards from people who stayed alive because I gave food to the neighborhoods during tough times."

"Yeah, so did Capone. That doesn't make him an honest businessman."

"But it does me. Look around. Do you see any machine guns?"

"No. But that doesn't mean your thugs don't have them in the trunk."

As he started to protest, I held up my hand. "Don't bother. I don't think you're involved. These people are sloppy and amateurish, not stylish like your thugs outside the door."

He ignored that.

"But it is possible you had something to do with whatever started all this. You're missing something. So is the kidnapper. Maybe it's the same thing, maybe not. But either way, paintings are mixed up in it. I keep looking around, but so far I'm coming up empty. And if you're not going to tell me what's missing, we're wasting our time here."

He looked out the window.

I continued. "Of course, you may be involved in all of it."

"You just said you didn't think I was."

I shrugged. "I've been wrong before. Maybe you're just having trouble getting good help."

I tried to read his reaction. There was none.

"And maybe your help is helping themselves."

He stared past me. "Maybe." He spun his chair and looked out at the harbor. "I have a proposition for you, Manning."

"Which is?"

He turned back to me. "I want to hire you to find out if someone is helping themselves."

I laughed. "Well, I'm sure that would be interesting. But I have enough problems of my own. I don't have time to look into yours."

He was quiet. I wondered what a crime boss thought about.

"What are your dreams, Mr. Maggio?"

He grinned, spread his arms wide and swept them across the room. "Look around you, Manning. I have all this. Why would I need dreams?"

I didn't look around—I just looked at him and slowly asked, "So, if this fulfills all your dreams, why do you need whatever it is you're missing?"

He stared at me for five seconds before he responded. "Because I don't like to lose, Manning." He pushed a button on his phone. "Miss Jenkins, please have Tommy come in."

As the door opened, he said, "We may talk again, Mr. Manning."

I handed him a card. "I have a phone."

When I got into the reception area, I paused and looked out the windows. That also gave me a view of the phone. It only took five seconds for one of the lines to light up. Trouble followed me wherever I went, and wherever I went people made phone calls when I left.

***

Tommy and I didn't speak during the ride home. That left me free to think. And what I thought was that Maggio hadn't known he had competition. I also thought he wouldn't be happy about it. It was a little after eleven. I'd be in Door for dinner. I headed north—again.

I saw the police cars as soon as we turned onto my street. There were two squads in front and Stosh's cruiser in the drive behind my Mustang.

We pulled up behind the squads and Tommy opened the door. He would have made a great chauffeur. He didn't seem bothered by all the police. The black sedan pulled away and I walked toward the house.

I got halfway up the front walk when the lieutenant came running out with his arms up in the air.

"Where the hell have you been?"

"What's all the excitement about? Did you get a call?"

"Did I get a call?" he yelled. "Yeah, I got a call—from my detective telling me you left two hours ago, but you forgot to take your car!"

I stopped five feet from him. I wanted to stay out of swinging distance.

"Oh, that."

"Yeah, that. Where the hell have you been?"

"Can we go inside? The neighbors have enough..."

He turned and walked inside.

I followed and explained what had happened. He had a lot of questions and I had few answers. And by the time we were done I realized I wouldn't make it up to Door in time for dinner.

Chapter 32

Almost everyone was sitting on the porch when I got there. Cletis, Peggy Sue, Ben, and Aunt Rose looked like they were spending an evening in Mayberry. Amelie was perched on the porch rail. I asked where Maxine was and heard a voice from inside.

"*Somebody* has to run the place!"

We all laughed.

"Where ya been, buddy?" Ben asked.

"Long story." I turned to Cletis who was holding Peggy Sue's hand. "Hello, Cletis. Nice to see you." I smiled.

So did he. "Nice to see you, too, Mr. Manning. Thanks."

I nodded. "Any cherry pie left?"

"I saved you a piece," said Aunt Rose. "It's on a plate in the kitchen."

"Terrific! Thanks. Ben. Let's chat in the kitchen. And Cletis, I'd like to talk to you, too."

"Tonight?" he asked.

"Yup. The sooner the better."

Ben and I sat at the kitchen table after I added vanilla ice cream to the plate.

"You going to share that?" Ben asked.

"You didn't have some?"

"More wouldn't hurt. What happened?"

I cut off a small slice of pie and got another plate and filled him in on my chat with Maggio. We discussed the possibilities.

"This keeps getting better," Ben said, eyeing the pie. "I have to wonder what Maggio has in mind."

"Hard to say, but I'm guessing somebody is *not* going to be happy."

"Good guess."

I finished the pie. "Speaking of happy, looks like a happy couple out on the porch. No problems this morning?"

"Well, Chief Iverson wasn't quite convinced, but he had to admit that Cletis' alibi checked out. And there's no complainant on the boat issue. Even if there was, it would be hard to call it theft since the owner had given him free use of it in the past."

"Did you ask him what he's involved with?"

He shook his head emphatically. "I told you, unless it's illegal I don't want to know about it. I'm not his therapist—not that he couldn't use one." He straightened in his chair and folded his hands on top of the table. "Spencer, this kid doesn't make good decisions. His thought processes are a bit on the slow side. But he's a good kid. And that girl loves him."

"I know that. Hopefully her love isn't misplaced. The heart isn't always a good judge of character."

I rinsed the plates and placed them in the dish rack on the counter by the sink. "Time for a chat with Cletis."

Ben gave me a pat on the shoulder. "Good luck. I hope you get some answers."

"You and me both."

***

When I opened the screen door onto the porch, conversation stopped. I thanked Aunt Rose for the pie and asked Cletis to take a walk. We followed a limestone path around the side of the inn that led to a gazebo at the back of the property at the edge of the forest. We chatted casually about the weather—it was still hotter and more humid than normal.

I motioned at one of the benches in the screened gazebo and we sat. Cletis looked nervous. His eyes were darting again. He looked down at the floor.

"Mr. Manning, I'd like to thank you for all you've done for us. I don't know how to.,,"

"That's okay, Cletis. Glad I could help. You've got a good girl in Peggy Sue."

He looked up. "I know. I'm not quite sure why she stays with me. That's why I..." He looked back down at the floor.

"You'd like to give her a better life?"

He nodded.

"Cletis, she said you were going to be rich. What did she mean?"

A wild turkey walked out of the woods and started crossing the lawn.

His face turned sad, and scared. "I just did it for her, Mr. Manning."

"What, Cletis? What did you do? Does this have something to do with the paintings?"

He looked crestfallen as he lowered his head and quietly said, "Yes."

"Cletis, there are two people dead. One is a good friend of mine. And another person has been kidnapped."

He stood up suddenly with clenched fists. "I got nothin' to do with that. You can't..."

I put my hand on his shoulder and sat him down.

"I'm not saying you do, Cletis. But I need to know what else is going on."

His eyes darted again.

"Okay?"

"Okay. I'll tell you." He watched the turkey until it walked into the woods and then started talking.

"I got a call at the store a coupla months ago. This fellow asked me if I wanted to make some extra money." He shrugged. "Why wouldn't I? So I said sure, depending on what it was. I told him I wasn't doin' nuthin' illegal. He said not to worry."

"Who did?"

He hesitated and then decided to talk. "The guy at the gallery in Chicago."

"Tony or Bloom?"

"Tony."

"So what did he want?"

"Not much. He just wanted me to switch two paintings when I framed them."

"What do you mean?"

"There was a list of paintings I was supposed to get from Johnson's studio. There were thirteen on the list. He told me to switch the frames on *Green and Blue* and *Harbor Nights*."

I thought about that and came up empty. "Do you know why?"

"He said he had overheard a phone conversation. He had only heard part of it, but said someone had bought *Green and Blue* and there was something special about the frame."

"And you framed the paintings?"

"All but that one. Mr. Gunderson said he'd frame that himself. He did it after I left."

"Curious. And you got the paintings from Kathleen's studio?"

"Yes."

"They were stacked and ready for you?"

"No. Miss Johnson isn't very well organized. They were all over the place. Some were stacked on each other."

"So you checked them against the list?"

"Yes. And put them in a crate."

"Could you have taken one that wasn't on the list?"

His eyes moved around the gazebo. "Well, I don't know."

"If you did, that would solve one of my problems."

He looked confused. "What do you mean?"

I moved nearer to him on the bench. "There were two paintings with similar names—*Green and Blue*, and *Blue and Green*. *Green and Blue* was on the list. *Blue and Green* wasn't, but it was missing from the studio. Do you remember those?"

"Am I in trouble?"

"I don't think so. Why? What happened?"

"I had put ten paintings in the crate. Then I found *Green and Blue*, but it was already checked off. I found the rest. I figured I had grabbed a wrong painting, but the crate was packed and it was near quitting time so I didn't want to unpack it."

"You brought them all back?"

He nodded.

"Did you find *Blue and Green*?"

"Yes. It was near the bottom."

"How did you know the names?"

"They were written on the backs of the stretcher frames."

"So why didn't you pull it out and bring it back?"

"I didn't want to get blamed. Mr. Gunderson got mad whenever I made a mistake. He said if I made more he would fire me."

"Didn't you think someone would find it sooner or later?"

"Well, no. I had a plan."

Aunt Rose came down the path with lemonade. I thanked her.

"So how much were you going to get for switching the paintings?"

"A hundred bucks."

I looked at him like he was crazy. "Okay, I'm really confused, Cletis. How is a hundred bucks going to make you rich?"

"Do I have to tell you?"

"You don't have to tell me anything. But there's still a lot about this that doesn't make sense. And if you did something that led to the murders and help me now, that will help you a lot."

He became agitated again, violently shaking his head. "I don't know about any murders."

"Okay, calm down, I believe you. What about the money?"

He looked around, like he was making sure we were alone and asked, "Do you have to tell anybody?"

"Not unless it's part of the other crimes."

Biting his lower lip, he continued. "I figured something big was happening and all I was getting was a hundred bucks. Why should Tony be the one getting rich? So I didn't switch the paintings the way he wanted. That was my plan. I switched the frames for *Green and Blue* and *Blue and Green* instead of the one he wanted. Then I could go down there and take *Blue and Green*, put it back, and keep the frame."

"Why not just take the frame of *Green and Blue*?"

"If I took it before they were shipped, it would be easy to pin it on me. But if I took it from Simmons, after they signed for it, then someone at Simmons would be blamed. No one would know I made a mistake and then I'd be the one getting rich."

I thought through his plan. It wasn't bad. "And that would take care of your mistake."

He nodded and took a long drink. So did I.

"But it fell apart." I kind of felt sorry for him.

"Yeah, when I found Mr. Gunderson I knew Tony had found out about the switch and come after me. He got Gunderson instead. I guess I didn't think of that."

"Or *someone* did. Why do you say it was Tony?"

"Who else would it be?"

"Cletis, this is so confusing that it could be twenty other people." I figured he wouldn't want to know one of those others was Larry Maggio.

He finished the drink and chewed on a piece of ice.

"Just a few more questions, Cletis. Do you have any idea what was so special about the frame?"

"No. But I looked at it when I switched them and it looked the same as the others to me."

"One more. When I was in the frame shop I looked around. There were several tools. You did the framing, right?"

"Except for *Green and Blue.*"

"Right. So when you're building a frame, what do you need a drill for?"

He spread his hands, palms up, and shrugged. "Nothing."

"You don't need a drill to make a frame?"

"No."

"But there was a drill on one of the tables. Any idea why?"

"Well, maybe Mr. Gunderson used it for the ducks."

"Maybe. Thanks for talking to me, Cletis. Do you have any questions?"

He shook his head. "Just thanks."

"Sure. You just take good care of Peggy Sue. And no more get-rich schemes."

"Gotcha. I will."

As we were walking around the front of the inn, Aunt Rose was just getting up from a rocker on the porch. Cletis went inside.

"Aunt Rose, is Maxine inside? I'm going to see if she wants to go to Wilson's for ice cream."

She glared at me and said in a stern voice, "She is not. She already went to Wilson's for ice cream."

I smiled. "Great. I'll walk over there." I started to walk down the drive.

"Spencer. She went with one of the fishermen."

That stopped me dead.

To my back, she said, "Spencer Manning, that girl loves you. If you care about her, tell her." A few seconds later I heard the screen door squeak open and then bang shut.

I continued down the drive, waited for a few cars, and then walked across the road to the bench by the harbor. It was the bench where I had sat when I first dropped Maxine off at the inn two years ago.

Chapter 33

got back to the inn a half hour later. Ben was sitting on the porch. I invited him to come to the cottage for a sleepover. After a smart-ass response, he packed a bag and followed me back across the peninsula. We talked over a couple of beers on the deck and I brought him up to speed on Cletis.

"This is beautiful, Spencer," he said as he looked out over the bay. "Does it belong to Rose?"

The breeze off the water was cool and the sky was clear and full of stars. I felt sorry for people who never left Chicago who would never see this sky.

"It did, partially. She owned it with Mom and Dad. We worked out the will and did some swaps and now it's mine—or it will be when the papers are processed."

He just stared out over the bay.

I smiled and said, "You can use it anytime you want."

"Thanks. I'll take you up on that. The painting situation is still confusing. Lots of people trying to steal something."

"Yeah. But what is the something?"

"What color were the frames?"

"Just natural wood with a varnish. Why?"

"Just thinking. It has to be something on the frame. That rules out gold coating of some sort. And it has to be the frame, doesn't it?"

"Yes. Paul suggested that she painted over a valuable painting, but the swap was made for the frame, not the painting. And Kathleen wouldn't have done that."

He nodded and scrunched his lips together. "So what else could there be with the frame? And who has it?"

"Well, there are three choices—Bloom, Vitale, and Maggio."

"How about whoever bought the painting?"

"My guess is that's Maggio. I don't think he'd care if one of his companies lost a painting. Just an insurance issue. But he cares about this."

"And you think he's involved?"

"I *know* he's involved in something. He confirmed that when he said he was missing something."

"And the murders and kidnapping?"

"Don't think so. Maybe he has a bad apple—someone freelancing."

"So if we set Maggio aside, which of the two do you like for the murders?"

"I'd have to lean toward Vitale, but who knows. He overheard a conversation between Bloom and someone else. So Bloom is in on whatever is going on. He may just be part of the plan or he might be the freelancer."

Ben nodded. "And Vitale tried to steal it from Bloom."

"Yes. And if I had to bet, I'd say Vitale is more likely to be violent than Bloom."

"Do you think Vitale knows the connection to Maggio?"

"If he does, he's nuts. But I don't think so. It took hours of digging through records for Stosh to find out."

"Do you think Bloom knows?"

"That's more likely, but I'm guessing not."

He set his beer bottle on the deck. "So, all that aside—where are the paintings? And there's one more possible thief—Kathleen."

"Well, technically not a thief. It was her painting."

"That's her friend talking. Maybe she *did* take *Harbor Nights*."

"There's no reason she would do that," I said emphatically.

"That we know of."

"Okay, let's say she did."

"Then what happened to *Blue and Green*?"

I shook my head. "Don't know. But if it was *Blue and Green* she took, she must have hidden it somewhere," I said. "And *it's* the one with the switched frame."

"But where?"

"Stop asking questions I don't know the answers to. I'm not buying that she took *Harbor Nights*. Bloom reported one stolen painting, *Harbor Nights*. I'm assuming that was taken by Vitale, thinking Cletis had made the switch. And then there's *Blue and Green* that Kathleen took."

"And *Green and Blue*?"

"That's one of the paintings that was already sold. It must have been picked up by the buyer who I'm assuming was Maggio, thinking that it was in the special frame. He then discovered he didn't get what he had bargained for."

"And how was Gunderson involved?"

"Cletis said that he framed all the paintings except for *Green and Blue*. Gunderson did that himself. Whatever is special about that frame was done by Gunderson. I figure he was part of the plan and got a cut. I also think that whatever is going on has been going on for a while. This framing procedure with the lists is pretty strange, but Kathleen's brother said that was the way they did it with his father."

"So, back to *Blue and Green*."

I sighed. "Okay. I think Kathleen thought the gallery was trying to steal her painting. She didn't know it was just a mistake by Cletis. She had four hours Friday morning before Rosie and Steele got there to hide it."

He looked puzzled. "How did she have four hours?"

"I'll pretend you didn't ask."

He chuckled. "Okay. So, we just have to figure out where she could have gone in four hours."

I laughed. "Anywhere. Four hours up here is a really long time. You can drive around the whole damned peninsula and stop for lunch."

"Everything's gotta be somewhere."

"Exactly. But there's a more important question."

He raised his eyebrows.

"Where's Pitcher?'

"Still no calls?"

"Nope. Very strange."

"Sounds like a loose cannon."

"Yup. And that's not good for Pitcher."

I picked up the beer bottles and tossed them in the garbage in the kitchen.

"What's next?"

"Man. I really hate to say it, but I think next is a visit to Simmons Gallery. I'm really getting tired of driving back and forth."

"I bet. I have another question."

"Shoot."

"I overheard Rose's comment about Maxine. Do you care about her?"

"I do. She's a wonderful woman."

"Then?"

"Then, things are a bit complicated."

"Because of what she was?"

I nodded.

"That matters to you?"

"No. Remember the wonderful part?"

"So?"

I took a breath, let it out, walked to the railing, and stared out over the bay.

"Everything would be fine. It has been. We have fun together. I liked holding her hand and wanted to do it again."

"So, what's the problem?"

"The first time we… You know." I shook my head. "It just, well, she'd wonder, or I'd wonder, or she'd be wondering if I was wondering. It would always be hanging over our heads. And then we'd both lose a friend."

"So, you can't forget that she used to be a lady of the evening?"

I stared out over the water. "I think I can, but I don't think she can."

Ben joined me at the railing. "You're not giving her that chance."

I didn't respond. There was more to it.

"Spencer, Rosie is a wonderful woman, too. What's your excuse with her?"

I turned to him and frowned. "Some sleepover this is."

He barely smiled. "Good night, Spencer."

"Good night, Ben."

Before I shut off the lights, I called Rosie and made a lunch date for Tuesday at Molly's to catch her up on the latest and maybe talk about us.

I went to bed with a few questions crossed off the list and several still nagging at me. Not all were about the case.

Chapter 34

ate an early breakfast on the deck, just cereal and blueberries, while watching various species of birds fly back and forth from the feeder to the evergreens. My neighbor two doors to the south pushed off from her dock in a canoe. We waved.

When I pulled out of the drive at seven, Ben was still asleep. I left him a note telling him to lock up whenever he decided to leave, and that he was welcome to stay as long as he wanted.

About an hour north of Milwaukee, I switched the radio to WGN and listened to Roy Leonard who followed Wally Phillips, talk radio at its best. The lead story on the ten o'clock news was the weather. Heat warnings were out, especially for senior citizens. The predicted high was one hundred—the record was one hundred two.

Forty minutes later, my pager beeped with my home number followed by the number nine—*call now*. I pulled off at the next exit. Lieutenant Powolski picked up on the first ring.

"We got a call, Spencer. He gave us a location and wants you there at three this afternoon. Rosie told me you have a lunch date at noon so I agreed."

"Where?"

"I'll fill you in at lunch. Are you coming home first?"

"No, going straight to Molly's."

"See you there." He hung up. I looked at the phone and sighed as I hung it up. I got a Coke out of the machine and walked slowly back to the car. It was too hot to move any faster. As I pulled out, I sighed. It may have been a sigh of relief—I couldn't talk to Rosie about us with Stosh around.

***

Stosh and Rosie were already there when I walked into Molly's, sitting across from each other in a booth. I slid in next to Rosie. We all ordered burgers.

"So? Fill me in."

Stosh emptied half a glass of water. "This heat is nuts. Male caller, wants you unarmed at a location up near Gurnee at three. Gotta drive your Mustang."

"Okay. But there's a big problem. I've got nothing to trade. I still don't know what everyone is looking for."

"Well," Stosh continued, "there are a few oddities. One is, it was a new caller."

"Geez, this just keeps getting crazier. So three different guys. Doesn't the same guy usually make the calls with something like this?"

"Yup." He finished the water. "Second, this guy was not nervous. He knew what he wanted to say and he said it."

I nodded.

"And third, he didn't *ask* for a trade. He just gave the location and time and said what you were looking for would be there."

"How does that make sense?"

Rosie looked concerned. "You could be walking into a trap, Spencer. You've pissed off a few people lately. Maybe you're the target."

I turned to the lieutenant. "Your take on this?"

"I agree with Lonnigan. This smells bad."

"How would they get me?"

The waitress brought the burgers. I reached for the ketchup.

"Any number of possibilities. I talked to the Gurnee police. It's a deserted motel far enough off of Highway 41 to be isolated—hidden from the road. There's nothing out there. Could be a sniper, or a bomb on a timer, or an ambush by someone in the motel."

I took a bite. Delicious. "Can you position someone somewhere?"

"Nope. I asked Gurnee. There's no way of placing someone without being seen if someone is watching. But the good part of that is there's no place for them to hide either, except in the motel rooms. So keep your eyes open."

"Good. Ambush or bomb. I feel much better. Any suggestions?"

Rosie answered firmly. "I suggest you not go."

I reached across the table and touched her arm. "Thanks. Glad you want me alive, but my gut feeling is this isn't a trap."

"Then what the hell is it?" Stosh spat out. "If the guy doesn't want a trade, what's the purpose?"

I shook my head. "Don't know, but I'd like to find out."

"Spencer." She moved her arm away from my hand. "Are you sure it's your gut?"

"What else would it be?"

"Guilt?"

"Guilt?" I replied.

"Yes. As I said before, you're not responsible for Pitcher being kidnapped."

"Hard not to feel responsible, Rosie. I led them to her."

"Not on purpose."

Stosh put down his burger. "If you two are done playing therapist, let's make some decisions here." He turned to me. "I could order you not to go."

"How could you justify that?"

"Interfering with a police investigation. And you may not come back."

Rosie laughed. "That's never stopped him before."

"Which?" asked Stosh.

"Both."

He ignored her. "What I *can* tell you is I don't think you should."

"Yeah, I don't think I should either."

"But?"

"But my gut says I should. There's something to be learned here." The burgers were gone. "Speaking of learned, I have some new information." I filled them in on the conversation with Cletis.

Stosh held up his water glass and the waitress walked over with a pitcher.

"So, that brings it into our lap," said Rosie.

"I think so, but still some options with the murders. And what the hell is with the frame?"

Stosh folded his arms on his chest. "And where is it? But first on the priority list is Pitcher."

They both looked at me. "I'm going. Instructions?"

"Yeah. Don't do anything dumb."

"Gotcha. Hey, have you guys played the tape of the calls for the boys at Simmons?"

"We did, both of them. And the girl. They were sorry, but they couldn't help."

"I bet they were. I'm gonna go home and shower off some of this heat."

I reached for the check but Stosh grabbed it first.

"Hey. Since when are you buying?"

"Since I'd feel bad as hell if I let you pay and then you ended up croaked."

I nodded slowly. "I'll take that—free food is free food."

He got up, leaving Rosie and me at the table.

She reached out and took my hand. "Spencer, do you want to talk about Kathleen?" She looked so sad. "You must be devastated."

"I'm trying not to think about it." I stared out the window. "You know, we've been around dead people. We've watched them die. I've never given it much of a thought—they were the bad guys. But…"

"I know. It's horrible."

I pulled my hand away and looked her in the eye. "I'm going to get him, Rosie. I'm going to…"

"Spencer. Revenge is never a good thing. Yes. Get him. But let the law take care of him."

I looked up and lost my anger. All that was left was sadness. The anger was easier to handle.

Chapter 35

I turned off Highway 41 just south of the Wisconsin border onto a dirt road, as instructed, and wound down a ridge through small stands of oak trees. I thought about whether I should be going off to the middle of nowhere by myself. I had weighed that and decided it wasn't the dumbest thing I had ever done, and I had survived that.

A cloud of dust billowed up behind my baby-blue Mustang. Around a bend, I saw deserted buildings left over from days when the area was a weekend getaway for those who couldn't afford the expensive real estate on the lake.

I scanned the ridge and the prairie beyond the buildings and saw no one and no place where anyone could hide.

Single, small, dilapidated wood units, with numbers one through six painted above the doors, stood next to a slightly larger building with a faded sign above the door that said "Office". On the other side of the office were three bare concrete pads with pipes stubbed two feet above the pad—expansion plans gone awry. Only one door was closed. Two were missing. The others stood open, inviting all of nature to join the desolation. Broken windows, missing shingles, and rotted wood left no memory of what must have been better times. A signboard precariously attached to the roof above the office advertised the Wayside Motel in faded red letters. The landscaping was dry, sandy soil and weeds—lots of weeds.

I stopped thirty feet from the office and got out of the car. The air was hot and dry, so hot and dry that my lungs hurt with every breath. The last weather report said we had tied the record. The only sound was muffled tires whining on the concrete highway the other side of the ridge. No one was in sight and there was no evidence that anyone had been there in quite a while. But the caller had specifically said that what we were looking for would be here.

I got out of the car, walked around the buildings and into every unit. Nothing. The cabins were empty. Every piece of furniture was gone. The walls were bare except for a crooked painting of a sad clown hanging in Unit 3. He was frowning and tears dripped down his cheeks. I guessed nobody wanted a sad clown. The remains of a nest in the cubbyhole of a bare counter in the office was the only sign of life. It was the right spot and I was exactly on time, but the place was deserted.

After waiting an hour, I left and drove back to the highway. I stopped at the first gas station and called Stosh, who answered with a hopeful hello.

"Nothing Stosh. The place is deserted. Not even a cockroach."

Lieutenant Powolski let out a worried sigh. "Spencer, I'm sure you will recall the many discussions we have had about the line that you'd better not cross or you'd have to deal with me."

"How could I forget with all your reminders?"

There was a long silence.

"Spencer, the line is gone—find her."

Chapter 36

got back to Chicago in fifty minutes, but it seemed like hours. My mind was racing as I tried to put all the pieces together. I failed. There were so many pieces, and I didn't know if they were all connected or parts of different puzzles. I thought of a friend who is a medical examiner who told me about a case where there were three bodies torn apart in an explosion. It was a puzzle and he had to figure out which body the pieces belonged to. He did, but it took a while.

Rosie and Steele were already in Stosh's office. He asked me to close the door behind me.

"Have you stopped the phone tap?"

The lieutenant pulled out his yellow pad. "No. I don't think it's over. I don't think whoever sent you north was part of the other calls."

"Then what?" asked Rosie.

She looked at all three of us with wide eyes and raised eyebrows, like she expected an answer.

I answered. "Too many pieces not fitting together, Rosie."

Stosh ripped five pages out of the pad and started writing. "Let's make a page for each crime and see what we have."

I suggested making one for the suspects. I figured it most likely that the same guy was behind everything. He ripped out another page and started writing.

The lieutenant spoke as he wrote. "William Bloom and Tony Vitale at Simmons, Edvard Gunderson and Cletis Mudd at Framed, and Maggio. And maybe someone we haven't met yet."

I leaned forward and looked at his list. "Two things. You've only got two Ds in Mudd."

I got a look of disgust.

I shrugged. "It's MUDDD. Might as well get it right. What if years from now someone's pulling up this case and they see MUDD. They're going to shake their head and wonder who screwed up the name. You going to sign that? Cuz I don't want someone thinking I…"

"What the hell's the matter with you?"

"Just saying. Second, there's a dead guy on your list."

He looked at me with daggers. "He may have been involved in whatever the hell is going on."

"I agree. But write deceased next to his name. What if years from now…"

"Shut up." He turned to Steele and Rosie. "Either of you have anything concrete to say?"

"Just note that Cletis has an alibi for Gunderson," Rosie said. "And maybe add Kathleen. It's unlikely, but she may have been involved somehow."

She glanced at me, probably expecting an argument. I had no doubts about Kathleen but I had been told to shut up.

Steele shifted in his chair. "I'm putting my money on Maggio. It would be nice to know who bought the painting."

"It would," said Stosh. "We're working on it. I'm guessing Bloom knows but he's not talking."

"Maybe I can get something out of him," I suggested.

Stosh shook his head. "You can try, but I doubt it. He got himself a high-priced lawyer."

"A gallery manager makes enough to afford a high-priced lawyer?"

"Probably not."

Rosie chimed in. "I wonder who's paying the bill."

"Me too," said Stosh.

"You been keeping an eye on Simmons?" I asked.

Stosh answered. "Yes. We set up across the street in an apartment above a cleaners."

"Anything unusual?"

"Nope."

"Anyone not showing up for work?"

"Nobody's missed a day."

"So if it's one of them, he has help to watch Pitcher."

We talked for an hour. Stosh wrote for an hour. He took another page to list what I saw at the motel. Steele made few comments. One was to ask what a painting of a clown would be doing in a deserted motel. I told him it was a sad clown—who wants a sad clown? He shrugged. At the end of the hour we didn't have any answers.

So I was back to none of it making any sense. I like things to make sense. Dad once told me that not everything does and sometimes you just have to give up and move on.

"Get to work, people," the lieutenant said.

I waited for Rosie and Steele to leave and turned to Stosh. "What exactly did you mean, the line is gone?"

He nodded toward the door. "Close it."

I did and sat down.

"Spencer, you sometimes do things that are legally questionable. So far, you haven't ended up in jail because you haven't crossed the line to definitely illegal. You've managed to dance around in the gray area and you do things we can't. And you get results. I want Pitcher back. If you find yourself questioning if what you're going to do is a little over the line, do it. I trust your judgment."

"And you'll back me up?"

He sighed. "Depends on what happens. But I won't be the guy in your face. And results speak pretty loud, especially if there's a cop involved."

I nodded. "You guys have nothing?"

"Nothing. This guy is either really good or really lucky."

"I'm going with lucky." I got up and announced that I was going home.

Chapter 37

There was a new man on the phones—Mike. But *man* was stretching it—he looked like he was still in high school. We introduced ourselves and chatted for a minute before I headed for another shower. The air conditioner was running nonstop.

Sometimes I think better while I'm taking a shower. I stand and let the hot water beat on my shoulders and clear my mind of everything except the problem at hand. So I was looking forward to some inspiration. I didn't get the chance.

I stuck my hand under the water. Just right. Then there was a knock at the door.

"Mr. Manning?"

"Yes?"

"We got a call. I told him you were indisposed. He's calling back in five."

"Okay. I'll be right out." I threw on a pair of jeans and a t-shirt. "What did he say, Mike?"

"Said he would let you talk to her and he'd call back in five minutes."

"I wonder if it was the same guy. Can you play it back?"

He did. The voice sounded familiar but I couldn't tell for sure. We could compare it to the others after the next call which came a few minutes later.

"Okay, Manning, here she is. Don't try anything funny."

A very timid voice said, "Spencer?"

"Yes. Brenda?"

"Yes. They told me not to say anything."

I recognized her pinched voice.

"Okay. Are you..."

"That's it Manning. I have what you want. Do you have what I want?"

"I don't, but I know how to get it."

"What the hell does that mean?" he demanded.

"That means I need a few days. There's too many people involved in this and I need to be careful."

"Okay, you be careful. But I'm calling back tomorrow, and if you don't have it by then you can say goodbye to the girl."

"Can't get it by tomorrow. I need till Friday."

"You think I'm stupid?"

"Listen, you made a lot of mistakes with this thing. I need to unravel your screw-ups to get what you want. I've got something going down Friday. Call back at one."

"If you're screwing with me, she's dead."

He hung up.

I took the deepest breath I'd ever taken.

Mike rewound the tape and played the first call. It didn't sound the same. But the second one did.

"Mr. Manning, I was briefed on what is going on. I thought the problem was we don't know what this guy is after."

"It is."

"But you figured it out?"

Another deep breath. "No clue."

He looked worried. "So?"

I smiled at him. "So, I've got till Friday to figure it out."

"Maybe you should skip the shower."

"Now I need it more than before. Call Lieutenant Powolski and invite him over to listen to the tape."

"Should I tell him..."

"No, just tell him we got another call and I'd like him to listen to it."

"Will do."

Now I was really hoping for an inspirational shower. I washed off the sweat, but I still didn't have a clue.

Chapter 38

Lieutenant Powolski walked in the door twenty minutes later with a serious look on his face and sat down at the dining room table where Mike was set up.

"So, tell me," he growled.

"Listen to the tape." I nodded to Mike.

When it was done, he looked at me with what I thought was relief. I had trouble enjoying his relief knowing about the shoe that was about to drop.

"So what happened since you left my office?"

"Well, I was about to take a shower when Mike knocked on the door and told me…"

"Spencer, cut the crap. How did you figure it out?"

Mike was looking up at the ceiling, perhaps hoping it wouldn't fall.

As I hesitated, I watched Stosh's face slowly change from hopeful to incredulous.

"Oh my God. You were bluffing."

"I had to. He sounded desperate. He wasn't going to buy '*I don't know what you're talking about*' again. I was lucky to get him to wait till Friday."

Mike was still looking up at the ceiling. It was still there.

"I guess there is that. But what next?" he asked calmly. I was surprised at his self-control. I expected an angry bull.

"Prayer?"

"Considering that we have nothing, we'll need more than that."

"I had to give him some hope, Stosh—to give Pitcher some hope."

"Yeah, you did okay, kid. But what the hell now?"

"I guess I take more showers."

He just looked at me like I was nuts. Maybe I was.

***

I called Rosie and invited her over to eat some pizza and watch TV. She said her other three dates had canceled so she'd be glad to.

I ordered an extra-large sausage, onion, and peppers that she and I and Mike finished without any leftovers. Mike assured us that he wouldn't be offended if we had beer while he drank a Coke. Rosie and I sat on the deck and watched clouds building in the west. It had only hit ninety and there was a slight breeze and a smell of rain in the air. Maybe a storm would cool things off.

"So, that's some limb you're out on," she said.

"Yeah, and there's a little troll sitting by the trunk with a saw. I don't like the look on his face."

She didn't smile.

"Rosie, I…" I wanted to tell her I cared about her.

"It's okay, Spencer. Just leave it alone. Some things just aren't meant to be."

"Seems to me that's up to the people involved. Is it something you *want* to be?"

Now she smiled. "I think it's more whether *you* want it to be. I've never changed my mind."

I was quiet while I looked at her. She was so pretty. "You are very special, Rosie. I just get close and then at a certain point, I…"

She smiled again, like a loving mother smiles at a clumsy kid. "I know. It's okay. I'm glad we're friends."

"Me too, Rosie."

A robin landed on the railing, looked around, and then flew away.

"Should we see what's on TV?" she asked.

"Sure."

I started to get up.

"Hang on a minute, Spencer. Wait. I'll be right back."

She was back in less than a minute with her wallet and pulled something out and handed it to me. It was a photograph of her and me at the academy. We had our arms around each other and were smiling big smiles.

"You saved this." I felt a wave of emotion wash through me.

"I did. And I look at it often. You mean a lot to me."

I was speechless and confused. Conflicting emotions and thoughts were bouncing off each other.

She reached out to take it back.

The emotions stopped and I just stared at the picture. I ran my fingers over the smooth paper.

"Spencer, you're acting weird. What's the matter?"

I looked up at her and then back at the photo. "Rosie, this is a photograph."

"Of course it is. Why are you acting so strange?"

"Because it's not a painting."

"Was there something in that pizza? What are you talking about?"

"When Stosh asked what I saw up at the motel I said there was a painting of a sad clown."

"I remember. So? It wasn't a clown?"

I gave her a serious look. "No, it wasn't a *painting*." I tried to visualize it. I hadn't been that close to it. "I think it was smooth, like this photo. And…"

"And what?"

I just looked at her. "And can you take a ride in the morning?"

"That's not what you were going to say."

"No. But I need to think some more. Can you?"

"I think so. I'll have to check in first. Where?"

"Wayside Motel."

We found Mike watching M*A*S*H. He was sitting in the recliner. We sat on the couch, not touching, but close enough that we could if we wanted to. I was glad Mike was there because I had no idea whether I wanted to or not. Or rather, a part of me did and a part of me didn't.

Chapter 39

Rosie called at eight Wednesday morning and said she could be at my place by ten. She was ten minutes late, but I wasn't in a hurry. I had until Friday at one—plenty of time.

It had rained overnight but it was still hot. Sunny and 85 at ten in the morning. We got to the Edens Expressway and headed north. Rosie looked lovely in beige slacks and a flower print blouse.

When we got to Lake Cook Road, where the expressway ended and turned into Highway 41, she asked, "Did thinking help?"

I moved into the left lane and passed a semi. "Maybe. But I want to be sure before I get anyone's hopes up."

She turned toward me in the bucket seat. "But there's a possibility about the hopes?"

"I don't know, Rosie. I'm taking it one step at a time. Even if I'm right about the clown photo, it may be nothing."

She stretched her legs out straight and flexed her feet. "Well, I've seen you be right more than wrong. I've got my fingers crossed."

"Thanks, Rosie."

"And Spencer. I've told you this before—I'm proud to work with you. You're a good man."

"Thanks. But I'll feel better if I can hear that from Pitcher."

"Understood."

We listened to WGN for the next half hour.

"It's less than a mile up on the right. You'll be amazed at how isolated it is. Once you get over a little ridge you might as well be out in the middle of nowhere."

"I've gotta tell you, Spencer, I'm getting excited."

I turned at the dirt road and followed it through a stand of oak trees. The motel came into view as we rounded a curve. The overnight rain helped keep down the dust.

Rosie's eyes widened. "Wow. It's like something out of a movie set."

"I wish I could have seen it back in its day."

"I like it better like this. Spooky."

I pulled up in front of the office.

"Mind if I walk around?" asked Rosie.

"Be my guest. I'll be in number 3."

Rosie walked into the office. I headed for the cabin wondering if the clown would still be there, or if I had ever seen it in the first place. Maybe it was the heat. Why would a picture of a clown be in a deserted motel? I hesitated in front of the door not wanting to find out I was nuts. I looked around the cabins. Nothing moved. There wasn't even a breeze to stir the weeds. I saw Rosie come out of the office and decided I had wasted enough time. I moved into the cabin, and there was the clown, just as sad looking as it had been the last time.

It was about eight by ten in a narrow, metal frame. I took it off the wall and ran my finger over the front. It was smooth. It was a photograph and it looked familiar.

As I was looking at the clown, Rosie came into the cabin.

"So that's the sad clown."

I nodded.

She came closer. "And it is a photograph."

"Yes."

"So you were right."

"Yup."

"And this helps somehow?"

"Maybe. It's a stretch."

She nudged a fat, orange and black caterpillar with her toe. It didn't move. "What's the maybe?"

"We have another stop to make."

"Is it is as cool as this?"

"No. It's Simmons."

"Oh. You're right. But there's something spooky about that place, too."

"Yeah, the people," I said with disgust.

I held the frame carefully by the corners so I wouldn't ruin any prints. But if my guess was right, there wouldn't be any prints.

***

We walked back to the car and I gently placed the photo on the back seat. I backed in a semi-circle and headed toward the highway.

"You're not going to tell me?"

"No, I'm going to show you."

With a mischievous smile, she said, "How mysterious. I would think you'd be more excited. You look awfully serious."

"Trying not to get my hopes up. I'll get excited when I can see Pitcher."

She lost the smile.

Traffic was light and we made good time back to the city. The Edens ended at the Kennedy Expressway and I headed toward downtown. I got off at Belmont and turned toward the lake and Clark Street. Traffic on Belmont was never good—lots of lights.

"You hungry?" I asked. It was a little after noon.

"Yup."

"Lunch or Simmons?"

"Are you kidding? I'm going nuts here!"

We had to park a block away. I asked Rosie to look at the photo.

"Got it in your head?"

"Yup."

"Okay, let's go."

It was a hot walk and I was trying not to show my excitement.

I held the door for Rosie and we went from heat to cool. We were met in ten seconds by Tony Vitale.

"Hello, Tony. Remember me?"

"Sure. The dumbfounded detective. But this time you bring a lovely lady."
He gave her an ingratiating smile. I was sure she was melted by it.

"Dumfounded. Nice. You keep a thesaurus in your pocket?"

He had no smile for me.

"You here for some reason?" he asked.

"Just wanted to show the lady Kathleen's paintings. Anything missing
show up?"

I got a hard glare and he left the room.

"Idiot."

"I'm hurt," said Rosie. "He didn't remember *me*."

"That's because I'm so distinguished looking."

"And modest."

Tony reappeared, making a show of straightening the paintings.

"Rosie, why don't you look around? I'll have a chat with Tony. Take a look
in the next room."

"We're not having a chat, Manning," he said bluntly.

"We already are."

I stood in front of a painting titled *Forest Trail*. Kathleen and I took many
walks in the woods. She was good at finding peace, at becoming a part of the
woods. They were some of my favorite times. I could feel her spirit in the light
filtering through the trees and streaking the path.

"This was painted by a friend of mine, Vitale."

"So what?"

"So, I'm going to find who killed her."

"I don't know about that. All I know is she was a thief."

"Sticking to that, are you?"

"Sticking to what? It's the truth."

"You said you saw Kathleen take *Harbor Nights*. You still sticking to that story?"

He looked irate. "It's not a story. That's what happened."

I moved to another painting. "You said you were just coming out of the
back room and she was close to the door. That's forty feet. You mean to say

from forty feet away, when you weren't expecting to see someone and were probably surprised, you were able to tell which painting it was?"

"I don't have to talk to you, Manning."

"No, but you may have to tell a judge."

"Well, that's not you, is it?" he spat.

I had the feeling he'd never be a fan of mine.

Rosie kind of floated through the opening to the next room with a jolly look on her face.

"Seen all you want?" I asked.

"I have. What a wonderful collection of clowns." She turned to Vitale. "You must spend a lot of time in there."

He tried to smile at her but didn't make it sincere.

I thanked him for his time and felt him glaring at my back as we walked out.

I hooked my arm around Rosie's waist. *"You must spend a lot of time in there."* I smiled. "Nice!"

"Thanks, but he didn't get it."

"Of course not—he's an idiot."

***

Back in the heat. Couldn't be good walking in and out of the cold all day. I was hungry and suggested we take a walk down Clark and pick something out. We found a French café and walked back into the cold.

We each almost emptied a glass of water and ordered a mixed plate of French cuisine for two. They didn't have cheeseburgers. And they didn't have Schlitz.

"So, notice anything in the clown room?" I asked with a tiny smile.

"Yes, your photo is a copy of a painting in the gallery. But what does it mean?"

"I'm not sure. But I don't think copy is the right term. I think it's a photo of that very painting."

"Are you saying someone took a photo of the painting and then hung it in the motel and then sent you to the motel?"

"That's what I'm thinking."

She looked confused. "Who would do that?"

I stared at her and raised my chin. "Someone who doesn't like to lose."

"Huh? Do you know someone who doesn't like to lose?"

I smiled. "I believe I do."

"Willing to share?"

"No. I don't think you want to know."

She cocked her head to the left and narrowed her eyelids to slits. "Okay."

The food arrived on a large serving dish and the waitress placed empty plates in front of each of us.

Rosie took a bite and said, "I overheard your conversation. Vitale isn't changing his story, but his story is full of holes. Why do you think he's lying?"

In between bites, I said, "Consider the missing paintings. We have *Blue and Green* and *Harbor Nights*. We know Vitale hired Cletis to switch the paintings in the frames between *Green and Blue* and *Harbor Nights*. He knew there was something about the frame for *Green and Blue*. So by putting that frame around *Harbor Nights,* he could then steal it any time he wanted."

Rosie was listening attentively while she ate.

"When he saw Kathleen, it fit his plan perfectly. He reported seeing her walk out with a painting, but because Cletis had put in the extra painting, there were still thirteen paintings in the crate. So Bloom just shrugged and wasn't concerned. So when Vitale stole *Harbor Nights* he just blamed it on Kathleen and told Bloom he must have miscounted."

"So Kathleen did take a painting?"

"Yes. *Blue and Green.*"

"And it's the one with the special frame?"

"Yup."

"Do you think Vitale knew what was special about the frame?"

"I don't know. But, if he's the kidnapper, he must know he doesn't have it. If he did, he wouldn't have taken Pitcher."

"And you have less than two days to figure it out." She looked worried.

There were several thoughts running into each other in my head. "Maybe I don't have to figure it out, Rosie."

"Of course you do. He's not going to give up Pitcher if he doesn't get his frame."

"Right. So I have to get Pitcher first."

"That'd work. And you have a plan for that?"

"I'm working on it."

"And I'm guessing you're not going to share."

"Nope. Again, you don't want to know." I finished what was on my plate. We were going to need a box. "Rosie, when Pitcher wasn't at the motel, Stosh told me the line was gone. I should just find her."

"What does that mean?"

I smiled. "He sometimes questions the way I do things. You've heard him tell me that there's a line and if I step over it I'll face charges."

"Oh, that line."

"Yup. He wants Pitcher back and is frustrated because you all aren't getting anywhere. So, the line is gone, but it's only gone for me—not you."

She looked concerned. "I don't like this, Spencer. Maybe the line has moved, but there's still a line. There are things the lieutenant can't help you with."

"I know, Rosie. I'm not going to do anything crazy."

"You mean anymore?"

I took a deep breath. "I want her back, Rosie."

"We all do."

"Me more. If she wasn't sitting at that table with me she wouldn't be in this mess."

"I know I'm not going to talk you out of that, but don't let it get in the way of being smart."

"Point taken. Ready for the heat?"

"Sure." She wiped her mouth on the white linen napkin and we pushed our chairs back.

We were both quiet on the ride back to the house, but my mind was racing. If I was going to do something, it had to be soon.

I gave Rosie the photo to take to the lab for prints. She gave me a hug in the driveway and gave me a look that I knew meant good luck. I grabbed the mail and headed inside.

Mike was sitting at the table and watched me drop the mail on the pile.

"You ever going to read all that?"

"Someday."

"Maybe there's something important."

I shrugged. "I check it after a week for bills that need paying—sometimes longer if I'm on a case. Mostly it's crap."

"I guess." Mike turned back to the TV.

I headed for the shower, and by the end of it I had made up my mind.

Chapter 40

sat on the deck for an hour, sipping the Schlitz I didn't have at lunch. Well, I sipped the second one—the first one I drank pretty fast. I watched the robins and let the facts bounce around and run into my ideas. I much preferred Kathleen's *Forest Path* painting to my thoughts. But there was one similarity. Kathleen's path was clear and well defined. I had a path, and it was clear, but it was built on a pretty weak foundation. Nonetheless, it was the only path I had.

I called the station at four and asked for Steele. He wasn't in so I left a message for him to call me as soon as possible.

Mike's relief showed up at five. I had never met her. Detective Connors. We chatted for a few minutes and I showed her around. I looked at the pile of mail and decided to go through it while I waited. I was halfway through the pile when the phone rang and Connors got ready. It was Steele.

"Hey, P.I. You called?"

"Yeah. Can I buy you a beer and some dinner?"

"I'm done for the day—sure."

We made plans to meet at Magoon's, an Irish pub on Irving.

We sat at the bar and ordered drinks. I ordered Harp and Steele ordered Glenfiddich. We took them to the table when one opened up.

"I heard about your phone call at one on Friday," Steele said.

I took a drink and looked at him with pinched lips. "Yeah, and if that call comes, Pitcher is a dead girl."

The waitress, who was about my age, apologized for the wait. It was their busy time. But we didn't have to wait that long and I wasn't in a hurry. I ordered shepherd's pie and Steele ordered beef stew marinated in Guinness. "Refills?" she asked.

Steele joined me with the beer. "You trying to get me drunk?" he asked.

"You may *have* to be to agree to my proposal."

The drinks arrived.

"Tell me, Steele. What does it mean if all this time has gone by and the police don't even have a hint about Pitcher?"

"It's not good. Probably means he has her holed up somewhere deserted, where nobody ever goes. We usually have connections on the street who get us something."

"You think he knows she's a cop?"

"Nope. I'm guessing this would be different if he did—and not in a good way."

"And how long do you figure he'd go along with me stalling him?"

"Not much longer. If he was a pro you wouldn't have had all this time."

"You're painting a pretty grim picture."

Steele took a drink. "I didn't paint it—it was already hanging up on the wall. I figure this guy is pretty desperate and has nothing to lose. He's already killed two people."

"Okay. We're on the same page. And now that I've got the pump primed…"

"If I'm the pump, what am I being primed for?"

I took a long drink. "For what I have in mind."

The food was delicious. I mixed the mashed potatoes in with the lamb and vegetables and ordered two more beers. And by the time we were done with the food I had laid it all on the table. He agreed, and he wasn't drunk.

I asked him a few questions. After some discussion, he gave me an address—4167 N. Pulaski. He said he'd need another person and asked if I had any suggestions. I told him no and especially not Rosie. I wasn't going to expose her to the possible official consequences. And I wanted to make sure he knew what those could be.

"Steele, I'm sure I don't have to spell out what the consequences could be. I feel awful even asking for your help, but I have no one else I trust."

He just laughed. Maybe it was the alcohol, but he had tossed caution to the wind.

"Manning, I love my job. But I walk into work every day thinking they'd be doing me a favor by firing me. I wouldn't miss this caper for the world."

I took a deep breath and nodded. I was glad to have him but, despite his words, I worried about the position I was putting him in.

"So we still need a person."

"No, we don't. I've got someone."

"Who?"

He smiled and finished his beer. "You don't want to know."

I knew I was stepping over the line and so did Steele, but he wasn't going to tell. And it wasn't far enough over that I would be in serious trouble. And if I was right, there wouldn't be any trouble.

Chapter 41

had no idea what to do with Thursday. I didn't get much sleep. My deadline was just over a day away and there was nothing else I could do. Everything depended on my plan and it was set up. Some of it was in Steele's hands and I had to count on him taking care of it. I didn't like having no options, but I couldn't think of another one. If the plan didn't work, Pitcher was dead. I had no doubt Vitale would kill her, perhaps in a fit of rage, like the way he probably killed Kathleen and Gunderson. I was sure they died when he got mad because they wouldn't, or couldn't, talk.

I started the day with an early errand and spent the rest it doing little things to take my mind off the situation. I looked at the pile of mail and considered opening more letters, but didn't. I set up the sprinkler and watered the flowers in the back yard. That was Mom's favorite hobby. It was mostly perennials so I just had to water and do some weeding. I ran some errands and got the Mustang washed, but nothing distracted me enough.

Mike was on the tape machine. He watched me every time I walked through the room. Midafternoon he said, "You seem nervous, and you look tired."

"I *am* tired. And I'm just frustrated. I like doing things. Just sitting and waiting isn't something I handle well."

"Yeah, I understand *that*. At least you get to leave. I have to sit here and wait for the phone to ring."

I nodded. "Yeah, that's worse. Must be pretty boring."

"It is. But when the call comes I can make a big difference."

"Good for you, Mike."

I spent the evening watching mindless TV with Mike's relief, but that didn't help either. As time went by, I just got more and more excited and wished I could make the hours disappear.

Chapter 42

Friday morning. I had a little less than five hours. Rain was forecast for later in the day. I got to Tony's apartment at seven just to make sure I wasn't late. I was also here yesterday at seven and had to wait an hour before he walked out of the front of his apartment building and got into his car about a half block away. It was now five after eight. It was 86 when I left the house, and I was warm with a light jacket on. I wore the jacket to cover my shoulder holster. I was parked in between the apartment and his car.

Traffic was light on the side street where Tony lived. Most people had already left for work so foot traffic was also light.

Ten minutes later, Tony walked down his steps and turned in my direction. Dressed in a beige suit and carrying a briefcase, he looked happy. That was about to end.

When he was two car lengths away, I got out and walked around the front of the Mustang. He glanced at me, looked away, and then glanced back. By the second glance he had lost the happy look. I stood in his path.

"What are *you* doing here?" he asked with a sneer.

"Came to take you for a little ride," I said calmly.

He laughed in my face. "What makes you think I'd get in a car with you?"

I pulled back the left side of my jacket. "This does."

His expression changed. He lost the swagger and froze. His eyes looked worried. But he had enough guts left to stand up to me.

"Come on, Manning. How dumb do I look? You're not going to shoot me out in the street with people just behind those windows. So why don't you just move on and I'll be getting to work."

"Vitale, I'd just as soon shoot you right here as anywhere else, and I don't care who sees or hears. I'll call the chief of police and have him watch. You killed two people. One of them was a friend of mine, just a kind soul painting and minding her own business until she got involved with you."

"Are you crazy?" His words were defensive and there was fear in his eyes. His hands trembled. "You've got no proof of that. I had nothing to do with her except to work with her paintings. Why would I kill her?" He bit his lower lip and his eyes were wide open.

"I don't know, but I don't need to know. I just need to see you dead."

"Who made you judge and jury?"

"Me." I patted my shoulder. "And I can back it up."

He didn't move.

"I'm offering you a chance to show me you didn't do it. But I'd just as soon shoot you without a chance."

"And that chance is?"

"Get in."

He straightened and stuck out his chin. "I'm not getting in without knowing where I'm going."

I shrugged and pulled my jacket apart. "Have it your way. I told you what your options are. You only have two, and they don't include any more discussion. Put your briefcase in the back seat."

He swallowed hard and slumped.

I motioned toward the passenger door and he got in as I stood on the walk. When he was in, I moved back around the car and got in.

"Okay, put on the seatbelt and slide both your arms under the belt. If your arms start to move, it'll be the last time."

He slid his arms under the belt and stared straight ahead.

I pulled away from the curb and headed north.

***

We said nothing as I drove. I'm sure he was trying to think of a way out, but he evidently found none.

Twenty minutes later I parked one address away from 4167 N. Pulaski, a five-story, brick apartment building. I handed him a key and told him to get out and walk into the building. I followed him. As we entered the vestibule, I stuck my gun in his back. He flinched.

"Open the door and start up the stairs."

When we got to the third floor, I told him to open up apartment C.

The door squeaked as it swung open and I pushed him in.

"Sit."

I holstered my .38 and looked around. There was the main room we were in, a small kitchen, and one bedroom with a small bath. The double hung window in the bedroom looked out over the rear alley and opened onto an iron fire escape.

He was still sitting in the chair when I got back to the living room. I stopped ten feet from him.

"We've got the girl, Vitale."

He looked shocked and almost jumped out of the chair.

"But she doesn't know who grabbed her. I'm expecting a visitor who should be able to clear this up. He saw the guy who kidnapped her. If he says it's you, you're dead. Take a look around—this may be the last place you ever see. When he gets here I need to talk to him first, so until he gets here, you stay in the bedroom. Get up."

I motioned him toward the bedroom, closed the door behind him, and waited. Ten minutes later, I went in to try and push him a little. He had to be in this with someone. I thought maybe I could get him to talk with an offer to go easy on him and blame the other guy.

The room was empty but the bathroom door was closed. I knocked. There was no answer. I tried the knob, but it was locked. I put my shoulder into the door and broke the lock. The bathroom was empty, too. I looked around the room and my eye stopped on the partially open window. I was sure it was closed when I walked through the room the first time. I looked out and saw an old man looking into garbage cans.

***

Sitting in the red chair in the front room of the apartment, I thought about the possibilities and tried not to worry.

At ten-fifteen the phone rang. A deep voice gave me an address—1140 W. Adams, just west of the loop off the Kennedy Expressway. I ran down the stairs and headed for the Kennedy.

***

Twenty-five minutes later I turned onto Adams and drove west. My palms were sweaty and I was sure my shirt was soaked. I pulled in behind a blue Chevy and stopped. I walked up to the passenger door of the Chevy, opened it, and slid in next to Ronny Steele.

"He went in a side door off the alley."

We were parked in front of an old brick building that looked like it was part warehouse and part offices. With broken windows and graffiti on the walls, it looked deserted.

"He's got her in the basement. The entrance is about halfway down the hall on the left. Her hands and feet are tied and there's tape on her mouth. There was another fellow who disappeared at the end of the first floor as I came in the door."

"You saw her?"

"Yup. I followed him. He was moving fast—never looked back. He's got her in a corner on a dirty mattress. Light bulb hanging from the ceiling. Lots of junk down there so it was easy to not be seen. And he wasn't looking—just in a big hurry to get to Pitcher."

"What did he do?"

"When he saw her he was furious. Told her she was dead. Then he went up to the second floor, into an office, and made a phone call."

"Could you hear?"

"Nope."

"Probably to one of his gang. That makes three that we know of."

"I agree."

"You didn't approach Pitcher?"

"No. I want to find out where the other guy is. I don't want to tip our hand."

"I don't want Pitcher dead, either."

"We have eyes on Pitcher. If someone threatens her, it'll be the last thing they do."

I didn't ask who.

"You sure she's okay? Cuz I'd just as soon kill everyone I see and worry about it later."

"Calm down, Spencer. She's as okay as she can be with tape on her mouth and all tied up. She'll last another hour."

I took a deep breath—and then another. "You've been in there. What do you suggest?"

"We make our way to the basement. As soon as we get in the side door keep your eyes open for the other guy. Vitale's had enough time to get back to the basement. One of us should stay at the stairs in case someone comes down, while the other moves over to Pitcher. Which do you want?"

"I want this bastard. I want to see the look on his face when he sees me."

"Okay. But we're not here for the look on his face—we're here for Pitcher."

"Understood."

We started out of the car.

"Spencer."

"Yeah?"

"This isn't the movies. If you need to shoot, shoot. No warnings. This isn't a negotiation—it's a rescue. These guys are bastards. And there are a hundred things we haven't thought of. This could go bad real fast. Always think."

"Got it." He cocked his head and gave me a look like he wasn't quite convinced. We walked down an alley strewn with trash, broken glass, and a paper bag in the shape of a bottle and drew our guns as we neared the door.

Chapter 43

Steele went through the door first and pointed to the left. I followed as he crept along the wall. About thirty feet farther he pointed to a door across the hallway. I nodded.

He opened the door and peered into the dark. He held his hand up. "Let's wait a few minutes to let our eyes dark adapt," he whispered.

It seemed like an hour, but a few minutes later he motioned to me to follow him. We slowly made our way down wooden steps. I could gradually make out detail in the room. It was about the size of half a football field and full of shelves and piles of various items, like old furniture.

When we got to the bottom, Steele pointed down one of the aisles and whispered, "All the way to the end."

I nodded and walked down the side of the aisle with my .38 at my side. I could faintly hear a voice which grew louder as I got closer. It was Vitale.

"Time to pee, bitch. I'm taking you in case I need you to get out of here, and I don't need you with a full bladder. Your boyfriend tried to trick me. I don't like being tricked. He obviously doesn't care much about you. I wonder how he'll like you dead."

I was about fifty feet away and I could see the corner where he had Pitcher through the shelving. One bulb hung from the ceiling. She was still lying on a filthy mattress, tied and taped. Her eyes were open but they looked dead. There was no emotion there, not even fear. I couldn't imagine how this had affected her. I wondered where he was taking her to pee, or *if* he was. If they were going up the stairs, this would get complicated.

Vitale pulled a six inch knife off of a shelf and told Pitcher he was going to cut the rope on her feet so she could walk. He bent and cut the rope. She barely moved her legs.

"On your feet, bitch."

She tried, but after lying down for days, there wasn't much strength in her legs.

He kicked her in the side. "Come on, bitch. I don't have all day."

I didn't just want to kill him—I wanted to kill him slowly and laugh while he screamed.

I knew we were at a disadvantage not knowing where the other guy was, but if he kicked her again I was going to shoot him and get it over with.

She finally got on her feet. Vitale stuck the knife in his belt. He pushed her, but not in the direction of the stairs. I was wondering whether to let him take her when I heard a shot from behind me. It sounded like a cannon as it echoed in the basement.

I turned in time to see a man's body fall in the aisle ten feet behind me. He was clutching a knife in his right hand. I had found the other man. He wasn't moving. I silently thanked Steele, but then realized he couldn't have made that shot from the bottom of the stairs. He must have moved.

It took two seconds to turn back to Vitale. He had turned in the direction of the shot, which was toward me, and pulled Pitcher in front of him. His eyes were wide open and his head jerked in different directions trying to find out what had happened. He called out to his friend, but, obviously, got no answer.

He was holding Pitcher with his left arm across her chest. When he brought the knife up with his right hand, I decided I had to do something.

I moved past the shelves and stood where Vitale could see me with my gun raised. He looked shocked.

"You! How the hell did *you* get here? Where's Crawford?"

I shrugged.

"You bastard!"

I thought I heard something behind me and wanted to make sure it was Steele. But I didn't want to let Vitale know there was someone besides me, and

I didn't want to take my eyes off of him. I could easily put a bullet into him from this distance, but that knife in front of Pitcher changed the game.

I aimed at Pitcher's chest. The hammer was cocked and my finger was pressed forward against the guard. I knew my gun, and the slightest touch of the trigger was all it needed.

"Look at me!" I yelled sternly. Vitale did, but I didn't care about him. I wanted Pitcher looking at me. She was. Her eyes looked scared but alert.

I started talking. I told him we could work this out—that we had no proof of the murders and he didn't need to add a murder charge to kidnapping. He didn't listen to reason, but I didn't think he would.

I thought back to a part of my academy training and hoped Pitcher had the same training and had been paying attention.

While I was talking, I sent her a message by blinking three times about two seconds apart. She blinked once, slowly, telling me she understood. I kept talking to distract Vitale. A few seconds later, she looked hard to the left and then back at me. Then she started blinking about a second apart. The third blink would be the trigger. Once. I took a deep breath. Twice. I was still talking. On the third blink, she twisted quickly to her left, pulling out of Vitale's hold. A split second later, I got off a shot before he could even *think* of stabbing Pitcher. He dropped to the floor with a hole in his chest.

I ran to her with Steele right behind me and took her in my arms. Steele bent over Vitale and said he was still alive but his breathing was gurgled. I didn't care.

I held Pitcher by the shoulders and pushed her away. She was crying. I was pretty close to doing the same. I holstered the gun and told her I would take the tape off her mouth. Apologizing, I told her I was going to do it fast and it was going to hurt. She nodded and screamed when I ripped it off.

She was sobbing as I went to pick up the knife to cut the rope that bound her hands.

"Hey," yelled Steele. "Don't touch that. Untie it."

I did. And then I pulled out my gun and walked over to Vitale. I stood over him and told him I was going to put him out of his misery for what he did to

Kathleen. I told him I had five bullets left and I was going to use them all. The first four would cause pain. The last would kill him. I told him I wanted to be there when he died and raised my arm.

Steele's stern, controlled voice came from behind me.

"Spencer, you don't want to do that."

I aimed at Vitale's left knee. Fear was all over his face.

"Oh, yes, I do."

"Spencer. We've got Pitcher and we've got this scum. If you do this, I guarantee you'll wake up one of these nights and feel guilty as hell. And, by the way, that will be in a prison cell."

I took a deep breath. All of me was trembling except for my gun hand.

"You got ten seconds, Vitale."

"Spencer."

I started counting down from ten and when I got to zero I pulled the trigger. The bullet tore a hole in the wood floor just below his crotch. I lowered my gun as his head rolled to the side and he took one last gasp.

I holstered the gun again and stood silently.

From behind me, Steele said, "Looks like you still may be going to prison."

I turned around, surprised. "How do you figure?"

"Looks to me like you scared him to death. And somebody is going to wonder how he got slivers in his ass."

Neither of us smiled.

Pitcher came over and put her hand on my arm. "Thank you, Spencer."

I put my arm around her. "Nice move, Pitcher."

"Yeah, I always wondered if that would work," she said with a smile.

"Good to see you smile."

"I didn't think I ever would again."

I turned to Steele. "And thanks to you for getting the guy in the aisle."

"Wasn't me, Manning."

I raised my eyebrows and remembered there was someone else in the basement. Steele nodded behind me with his chin.

Leaning against one of the shelves was Chief Iverson.

"Well I'll be damned." A big smile spread across my face and I laughed.

I walked over to him and held out my hand. "Thanks—Chief."

He took off a glove and shook my hand. He nodded with a tiny smirk on his lips and said, "By the way, the guy in the aisle is dead, too."

I nodded.

Iverson put the glove back on and handed the gun to Steele who took it in his right hand to put his prints on it.

Steele took over. "Iverson, get the hell out of here. Manning, let's get back to the car and get some help here and an ambulance."

I turned to Pitcher. "Think you can make it up the stairs?"

"I think so, as long as we go slow. But..."

"What?"

She laughed. "I really do have to pee."

"Do you know where the head is?"

She nodded to her left. "Over there about halfway down the wall."

"Okay. I'll walk you to the door. Steele, why don't you go make the calls."

He shook his head. "I'll wait. We all stick together. I don't want any surprises."

"Okay." I looked around. "Where's Iverson?"

"Anywhere but here. Let's go." As we left, we laid out our story.

***

When we got to the street, I put Pitcher in the Mustang. Steele had a radio in his car and used it to call for an ambulance and the police.

A fire department ambulance arrived first and took control of Pitcher. Ten minutes later, a paramedic assured me she was in good shape, but they were taking her to the hospital.

She thanked me again and gave me another hug.

Squad cars started to arrive right after the ambulance. Fifteen minutes later, there were twelve cars in the street and alley. Lieutenant Powolski and Rosie were the last to arrive. A Captain Marks and two detectives from the third district had talked to me and Steele and heard the basic facts. He told us there would be a lengthy interview. I should be at the third district station Monday morning at nine.

When the lieutenant and Rosie arrived, Captain Marks was walking away from me. Stosh walked up to him and chatted before he came over to me.

"Do I want to know?" he asked with arms outstretched and his palms up.

"It'd make a great story for your grandkids."

"Since I don't have any of those, why don't you just give me the story you told the captain."

Steele and I had already agreed on what we were going to share. We told Pitcher to tell exactly what she saw, but told her we'd appreciate leaving Iverson out of it. She said she'd say she was rescued by Superman if we wanted her to.

"Not much of a story. I got a tip and we found Pitcher in the basement. Vitale pulled a knife and I shot him. Another guy pulled a knife on me and Steele shot *him* before he could stab me in the back. Pretty simple, really."

"Sure. Nothing to it."

"Yup. Nothing to it. I suggest you go through Vitale's apartment and see if you can tie him to the murders. I'm pretty sure he's our man."

"We're taking his place apart as we speak. And going to have a chat with Bloom."

He held out his hand and I shook it. He nodded. That nod said more to me than any words could have.

"Let me know if you need help with anything," Stosh said as he walked away.

Rosie had been waiting off to the side. She came over and put her arms around me. "You're the best, Spencer. Words can't thank you."

"Don't need to, Rosie. I got lucky."

"Right. Didn't your dad say that lucky people made their own luck?"

I smiled. "He did."

She smiled back. "Someday you'll have to tell me how you made this luck."

"Someday. But I need some more—still don't know what this was all about."

"And you may never." She walked away and I went over to Steele.

"Dinner tonight at Magoon's?"

"Sure. This time I'll buy. See you there at six."

"Right."

I got into the Mustang and headed home for a hot shower.

Chapter 44

When I got home, Mike was dismantling the recording equipment and packing up.

"You made the news," he said with a big smile. "Nice job."

"Thanks, Mike."

"Looked like the whole force was out there."

"Yeah. Quite a crowd."

"Is she okay?"

"They took her to the hospital just to be sure, but she was laughing and walking, so I think she'll be fine. Pretty tough lady."

"I guess. I can't imagine going through that."

"I'm going to get a shower. Thanks for your help here, Mike."

"Sure, just doing my job. But there's something…"

"What?"

He scrunched up his face. "I hope you won't mind. I was bored, so I kinda looked through the pile of mail here on the table."

I laughed. "Did you pay the bills?"

"No, but there's one near the bottom you should take a look at."

"There is?"

He nodded. "It's from Kathleen Johnson."

I took in a sudden breath. "Jesus. Guess I should do something about ignoring the mail. Thanks, Mike."

"Sure. Take care, Mr. Manning."

"You too, Mike."

After he left, I found the envelope and stared at it for a minute before opening it. There was one piece of unlined paper inside with one word on it in capital letters: PIRATES. I knew where the painting was.

***

Steele was waiting for me at the bar, sitting next to Iverson. He said he had put our names in and it would be twenty minutes more. I ordered a beer. They had Glenfiddich.

The bartender put a glass of Harp in front of me and Steele raised his glass to clink mine. Iverson joined in.

"I gotta admit, you guys pulled off a helluva surprise." I took a drink and put on my best sheepish look. "And, uh, I have an apology, Chief."

He sipped his whiskey and said, "Don't worry about it, Manning. You made it up to me with the look on your face in the basement." He took another sip. "Nice shooting, Manning. That took some guts."

"I pulled the trigger, but the guts weren't mine. They were Pitcher's."

He nodded slowly.

"I have some questions," I said.

"Shoot." Steele set his glass down.

"I would have loved to have seen Vitale climbing out that window."

Steele responded with a big smile. "It was classic. He was going like a bat out of hell with a smug look on his face."

"Steele, the only hole in the plan was following him. How did you work that out?"

"Well, kid, there were plenty of holes—lots of things that could have gone wrong. We got lucky. But that part wasn't a hole."

"How did you know you wouldn't lose him? Tough to follow someone on foot when you have a car."

They both laughed. "When he came running out of the alley there was a taxi just letting out a fare at the curb. Vitale hopped in. I just tailed it."

"I guess we did get lucky. But what if you lost them?"

Steele looked pretty smug. "Luck had nothing to do with it."

"Why not?"

Iverson raised his glass. "Because I was driving the taxi."

"Close your mouth, kid," said Steele.

"I gotta admit, when I told you to work that out, I was worried. That's brilliant."

"Yeah, one of my better plans."

The hostess called Steele's name and we moved to a table. After ordering, I continued.

"I've got an interview with Captain Marks Monday morning. What do you think the fallout is going to be?"

Steele slowly shook his head. "Nothing. If we can make it make sense, that's all they're looking for. And the simple story makes plenty of sense."

"Sure. As long as they don't start asking questions. Like who gave me the tip, or how did we happen to meet up with Vitale."

"Nobody's going to ask those questions. The only person who could throw a wrench into this is Vitale and he ain't talking. Don't worry, Spencer. Just stick to the basic story, which just happens to be true. They've got our prints on the guns and the bullets match up with the victims. Everything wrapped up."

"I guess. Good thing the chief here wore gloves."

"All part of the plan, kid. He was never there."

The food arrived and we dug in. I was hungry.

I turned to Iverson. "Anything new up in Door?"

"I have Paul scouring the harbors looking for evidence that Vitale rented a boat."

"What about Grizzly's boat?"

He shook his head. "I'm betting we're not going to find it anytime soon. I think it's somewhere on the bottom where they found her. Whoever did it, killed Kathleen, took her out on the boat, and sunk it.

Steele said, "I'll get copies of Vitale's picture and chief can distribute them. If he did it, and that's where my money is, he rented a boat. We'll connect the dots sooner or later. And I'm sure they'll come up with something at his apartment. Guys like him aren't very smart. There'll be evidence lying around somewhere."

"I have something," I said in between bites.

"And that is?" Iverson asked.

"I think I know where the painting is."

"Which painting would that be?"

"*Blue and Green*. The one Kathleen took from Simmons."

"And where would that be?"

"I'll let you know after I find it. So far it's just a hunch."

Iverson shook his head. "You P.I.s. We gotta dot every *I* and cross every *T* and you get to run around with hunches. And by the way, you wouldn't happen to know where Muddd disappeared to, would you?"

"That depends. What do you want him for?"

"Just questions about Gunderson."

"I thought he had an alibi."

"Yup. It's solid. He's not a suspect, but he might be able to help."

"In that case, he's at the Harbor Lantern Inn."

"And how do you know that?"

"Because I'm the one who *disappeared* him. And he didn't disappear, just moved. He and his girlfriend were going to be evicted for not paying the rent."

"Hmmm. So you made poor Rose an accomplice."

"Yup. She'll do hard time if she has to."

We both smiled.

"He might be able to help you with placing Vitale up in Door," I suggested.

Iverson wiped his mouth. "He might at that."

"So what's on the agenda, Manning?" asked Steele.

I put my fork down and declared dinner over. I had shoveled in all I could. "I'm going to head north in the morning and check out my theory. Then back by Monday for the interview. I wonder how long that will take."

"Not long at all," said Steele. "You're at nine. They asked me to be there at ten. Won't be a problem."

"I hope you're right."

The waitress brought the bill. Steele paid.

On the way out, Iverson asked me to let him know about the painting. I said I would.

I spent an hour on the deck when I got home, mostly thinking about Kathleen. We never would have been able to live together, but I loved her. She really was just a kind person who loved to paint. What a shame. Killing Vitale brought some closure, but it didn't take away the sadness.

I slept well for the first time in a week.

Chapter 45

Before I left Saturday morning, I called and invited Maxine for a boat ride after lunch. She asked me to hold. A few minutes later, she came back and told me Peggy Sue would cover for her.

I stopped at Coyote for a sandwich and homemade pea soup, and chatted for a few minutes with Paula.

The thermometer on the Ephraim bank read 90 degrees and I may as well have been in a sauna with the humidity. There was a smell of rain in the air. I parked in the lot at the inn, walked across the street to the marina, and rented a boat for the afternoon.

Aunt Rose was waiting for me on the porch. "Well, if it isn't the famous Spencer Manning!"

With one foot up on the stairs, I said, "Aw shucks, ma'am."

"Come here and let me give you a hug," she said with a big smile.

She put her arm around my waist and walked me into the inn. Maxine was behind the desk.

"My hero!" She ran around the desk and threw her arms around me as Aunt Rose moved away smiling.

"We're very proud of you, Spencer," said Rose.

"Well, I did have help, you know."

Aunt Rose gave me a kiss on the cheek and said, "I've got work to do. You two kids go have a good time." She winked at me.

Maxine ran up the stairs saying she needed to get a hat and sunglasses.

***

By two, we were pulling away from the dock in a 24-foot Bayliner. I brought it up to twelve knots as we moved through a slight chop in Eagle Harbor.

"Where are we going?"

"Well, that depends. First stop is Chambers Island. But we may stop at a couple others after that."

"Depending on what?"

"On whether I find what I'm looking for on Chambers."

"And what are you looking for?"

"Pirate treasure."

She came up and sat next to me at the helm and just gave me a questioning look.

I made way through the boats in the harbor and came up to twenty knots as we moved into Green Bay. We passed Horseshoe Island and headed west around the point of Peninsula State Park.

"Take a look to your left."

"Is that the tower I climbed?"

"Yup. Keep looking. Kathleen and I spent some wonderful summers up here. We'd beach a boat on one of the islands and have a picnic. She'd paint and I'd read mysteries and fall asleep in the sun. We…"

Maxine pointed to port and yelled, "There's the lighthouse!" as we passed the Eagle Bluff light. "I'm sorry, please continue."

I laughed and pointed out our destination, Chambers Island, about five miles in the distance. The heavily forested island, and the second largest of the many in the county, loomed green and imposing in the distance. I pointed out the Strawberry Islands as we made our way between them. One was just a bar of sand, a sunning spot for birds to dry their wings in the sun after diving for fish.

The trip across the open waters of the bay was pretty calm. With a ten- to twelve-knot wind out of the northwest, I could angle into two- to three-foot waves. As we came into the lee of Chambers Island, the water flattened out and, after telling Maxine that we were going to take the circular tour of the island, I continued and brought her up to date on what I knew about the frame situation and the missing painting of *Blue and Green*. She was most interested in the clown picture and my visit with Maggio.

"Weren't you scared?"

I laughed as I swung in a few hundred feet from shore and slowed to twelve knots. "I was a bit worried at first. Wouldn't call it scared. But I soon realized they meant no harm. As he said, it could have been handled differently. So I relaxed and wondered what Maggio wanted and what pieces I could add to the puzzle."

She didn't respond and I could see the wheels turning as she thought. I loved watching her think, and her thoughts had been right on target. She was a smart lady.

I was moving clockwise around the island so she could watch the scenery and talk in my direction at the same time.

"So, do you think Maggio had something to do with the clown picture?"

"I'd put money on it."

"Why would he do that?"

I pointed out an eagle in the trees. "Because he doesn't like to lose, and nobody likes being double-crossed."

"So, Vitale was stealing from the mob?" she asked with surprise.

"That was the result. We'll never know, but I'm betting he didn't know Maggio was involved. He just overheard a conversation between Bloom and whoever was on the other end of the phone."

"And you think that was Maggio?"

"Hell no! He has people to do his dirty work."

She thought some more and then touched me on the arm with a tiny smirk. "You mean like you?"

I smiled back. "Exactly."

The smirk was still there. "So he offered to pay you to work for him and you refused. But he got you to do his dirty work for free."

As we came around the south tip of the island, we turned straight into the wind and the waves picked back up.

"That's the way it worked out. But I choose not to think of it as dirty work. He did the legwork and discovered that Vitale was stealing from him. He just pointed me in the right direction."

"Why didn't he just tell the police about Vitale, or get him himself?"

I laughed. "He's not the type of guy who talks to the police. I gave him an interesting option. When I turned him down, he knew I was straight but was after whoever killed Kathleen. And me getting Vitale was a lot better for him than having one of his guys kill the guy in an alley. His hands are clean."

"So you think he wanted you to kill him?"

"I think that was preferable, but he would have been happy with Vitale doing a life sentence, too."

"So he planted the clown picture and took a chance that you'd figure it out. Seems to me there would be more direct ways of letting you know."

"Probably, but I have the feeling this guy likes to play games. I also have the feeling he didn't have any hard evidence. He was just putting two and two together and getting Vitale. He left it up to me to see if Vitale was the guy or not. And he hoped I would link the clown photo to Vitale's clown exhibit."

"What if you didn't figure out the clown clue?"

"Then I think there would have been more, perhaps less subtle." I pointed to starboard. "As we come around that clump of trees, keep your eyes open and tell me what you see."

In a few minutes, her eyes opened wide and her jaw dropped as she pointed toward the island. "Am I going crazy? That's the Eagle Bluff Lighthouse."

I laughed. "Well, as close as you can get. That's the Chambers Island light. They're almost twins."

"How cool is that! Does it still work?"

"No, it was shut down in 1961."

"How fun it must have been to live there, especially for a kid."

"Sometimes. There's a great book called *Lighthouse Families* by Cheryl Roberts. It's in the library at the inn. Some families thrived and became very close. Others were broken apart. Just depended on the people. Many keepers were alcoholics and there were suicides, too, when the job got too tough."

"How sad. So what brings us to Chambers Island?"

"I told you—pirate treasure."

She gave me a disgusted look. "Pirate treasure. How gullible do I look? Has everything you've been telling me been a figment of your imagination?"

I laughed. "No, everything's true, even the treasure. Kathleen and I did a lot of exploring and found lots of hiding places, most of them just small openings in the rock, but there were some caves in the limestone big enough to move around in. We hoped to find treasure but we never did. So we left our own time capsules hoping someone else would find them someday. We pretended we were pirates."

"And what does that have to do with this trip?"

"Kathleen was warned that the police were coming that Friday morning. That gave her several hours to hide the painting."

"That's the one that Cletis switched the frames on, right?"

"Yes. And the one that holds the pirate treasure."

She was thinking again. "And you think she came out here and hid it in the cave?"

"That's what I'm hoping."

"And you remember where the cave is?"

"I think I can find it. There's a lake on the east side of the island. Mackay-see Lake. To the west of that is a smaller lake called Mud Lake. In between is a hill of limestone and in that hill is our cave."

As we rounded the north point, I angled in toward the island and a short, wooden dock came into view.

"Are there people here?" asked Maxine.

"There are some cabins and some people live here in the summer, but none permanently."

I told Maxine to throw a line over one of the dock posts and showed her how to tie it to our cleat. I grabbed a flashlight and we stepped onto the pier as the boat bobbed gently in the swells.

Chapter 46

t only took ten minutes to hike to the eastern shore of the lake along a footpath
that rose above the marshy land.

"This is beautiful, Spencer."

"It is."

"I can see why you came out here."

I pointed out two islands in the lake.

"That's amazing. Islands in a lake on an island in a bay. Wow."

"Yes, nature is wonderful. All you have to do is look around."

"Well, a bit more than that. It took some effort to get here. I would never
have known this existed if it weren't for your pirate treasure."

"Ah, yes." I looked around, remembering what it looked like ten years ago.
It hadn't changed much. "I've always had a strange feeling knowing that I was
looking at something few people would ever see."

We walked around the south end of the lake and headed west toward Mud
Lake. I thought of Cletis. Only one D in the lake name.

Maxine stopped to look at a flower.

"So, what if it's not there?"

"There are other possibilities."

"And what do you think is going on with the frame?"

"No idea. Hopefully we'll soon know."

It took a little bit of hunting, but I soon found the overgrown entrance to the
cave. We had to stoop to walk in. As soon as we did, the temperature dropped

in the natural air conditioning of the limestone cooled by the groundwater which was only a few feet below the ground.

The cave wasn't very deep. I shone the light on the back wall illuminating a few bats hanging from the ceiling. I didn't point those out to Maxine. I moved the light around the cave and saw nothing besides cave.

"This is very cool, Spencer."

The floor of the cave was dirt and pieces of rock. I pointed out an opening ahead on the left and beckoned for her to follow me. I held my breath as we reached the opening and shone in the light. Propped against the left wall was the painting.

As my light found it, Maxine exclaimed, "There it is, Spencer! You're a genius."

"I doubt that. Just a logical assumption."

"Well, I'm impressed."

I gave her the light and picked up the painting. I instantly felt sad. I was holding a connection to Kathleen and remembered all the wonderful times we had shared. Maybe I was too selfish and stubborn about our relationship. But the logical part of me realized I was thinking with my heart and there was much more to it than that. Regardless, I missed Kathleen.

Maxine was quiet. I think she realized what I was feeling.

"Let's go, Maxine." She turned and led the way out.

When we got back to the boat, we sat on the edge of the pier and looked at the painting. I decided to hang it in the cottage. I looked at the frame and didn't see anything meaningful. I handed it to Maxine and she couldn't find anything either. The mystery remained.

"I have a question, Spencer."

"Shoot."

"Why did Kathleen just write PIRATE? Why not just explain where the painting was?"

"Good question. If you knew Kathleen, you wouldn't have to ask. Several reasons, I'm guessing. She loved games. We would constantly try to stump each other. But more importantly, I think she wanted to make sure no one else would be able to find the painting. If she thought someone was trying to steal it, she might also have considered someone getting ahold of the letter. So this way I'm the only one who would know what it meant."

"Pretty smart."

"She was very smart. Too smart to have been done in by Vitale. I'd love to know how that happened."

We watched the waves for a few minutes.

"Let's go, ma'am." I took her hand and helped her up. She stowed the painting, let go the lines, and we headed back to Eagle Harbor as the sun slipped lower in the west. The breeze from the moving boat felt good in the heat of the sun as a few puffy cumulus clouds floated across the blue sky.

***

We docked the boat. Maxine stayed at the inn and I drove over to the Ephraim police station. Paul was there alone. I asked him if he had any news.

"Not yet, but we're trying. Photos have been distributed to all the marinas and put in the papers, and I talked to most of the staff at the marinas. But he could have driven a boat up from somewhere south and docked by the hour instead of renting a boat from here. The guys on the docks can't remember everybody. I also passed his photo out at the gas stations. The sheriff is covering down in Sturgeon Bay."

"Okay, thanks. Gonna have to get lucky. What's my buddy Iverson been up to?"

He shrugged. "Haven't seen him for the last few days. Said he was going to do some fishin'."

"Good for him. Maybe that'll help his attitude."

"Hmmm. I doubt it. He's been fishin' before."

I laughed. "I bet he has. Take care, Paul."

I got up to leave.

He looked serious. "Hey, Spencer. Nice job." He held out his hand.

I took it and nodded. We didn't need any words, but I was dying to tell him about Iverson.

***

took Maxine and Aunt Rose out to the Greenwood for dinner and filled Rose in on what I could that wasn't covered on the news. She was glad I was here to tell her about it. So was I. Maxine asked a few more questions.

"So, are you staying for a while now that you got him?" asked Aunt Rose.

I shook my head and finished chewing a bite of steak. "Only if till tomorrow afternoon is a while. I have an interview Monday morning about the incident."

"Interview?"

"With the cops. They want to know what happened."

Aunt Rose looked concerned. "Is there going to be any trouble?"

"I don't think so. It was really pretty simple. And we did get Pitcher back and there's one less bad guy walking around."

She took a deep breath. "Well, call me when it's done so I can stop worrying."

I said I would.

Maxine was just sitting quietly, listening, and eating salmon.

We all had cherry pie and ice cream for dessert and went home well fed.

Chapter 47

It was dark by the time I pulled up in front of the cottage. I had put a timer on the light in the living room and it was on. I decided to take a better look at the frame.

I placed the painting on the kitchen table with the light shining down directly on it. I looked at every inch of the frame and found nothing. I got a Schlitz, popped off the top, and got my tool kit. I pried the fasteners from the edges and pulled the painting out of the frame. I looked at the inside edges and again found nothing.

Maybe there was something in the joints. I got a small pry bar and considered forcing the pieces apart, but decided that would damage the wood and, since I had no idea what was important, I decided not to do that. I looked at it for a minute and then picked it up and tried to pull apart a corner. It didn't budge. Cletis had done a good job on the frame.

I wasn't going to be beaten by a frame. I looked at it some more and then held it out from my chest by opposite corners and squeezed. In a few seconds it started to collapse slowly and then the corners gave way and the rectangle became a parallelogram. The corners were still attached, but now I could pull them apart. Before I did, I marked the parts with four letters—B,T,L, and R, so I could put them back in the same relative position.

I looked carefully at each end and still came up empty. There was nothing there. Maybe Cletis had made a mistake with the painting.

I called the inn. Maxine answered and I asked for Cletis.

"Hello, Mr. Manning."

"Howdy, Cletis. Things going okay?"

"They sure are. Your aunt has been so nice to us, and I found a job. I start Monday at the marina in Ellison Bay. I'll just be a dock hand at first, but the manager said he'd move me up since I have experience with boats."

"That's great, Cletis. Good luck. I have the painting *Blue and Green* and I'm not seeing anything special about the frame. Could you have been mistaken about which painting you switched?"

"No, it was *Blue and Green*."

I was clutching at straws. "How did you know it was *Blue and Green*?"

"Simple. The names are on the back of the stretcher frames."

I turned the pieces over and there was the name on the one marked L. I thought some more. "Maybe the names got rewritten somehow. Would you remember the painting?"

"I think so. I liked it more than the rest."

"Okay. I can be there in twenty minutes. Would you take a look at it?"

"Sure."

I set the painting and the frame in the back seat and headed back to the inn wondering what I was missing. Then I thought of another possibility. Vitale was cheating Bloom and Cletis was cheating Vitale. Maybe there was another player. Maybe Gunderson had cheated all of them and hidden whatever it was in his house.

***

Cletis and Peggy Sue were waiting for me on the porch. They were sitting on the wicker bench holding hands. We exchanged hellos. Peggy Sue looked happy.

I was holding the painting with the back facing Cletis. "Let's go inside, Cletis, where there's good light."

"Mind if I come?" asked Peggy Sue.

"Not at all. The more eyes the better." Maxine was working at the reception desk. I asked her to get Aunt Rose.

They both came out of the kitchen as I set the painting upside down on the table.

"Okay, Cletis. I'm going to turn it over. I want you to try and remember *Blue and Green* and tell me if this is it."

I turned it over.

In less than five seconds, he nodded. "That's it."

"You're sure."

"Yes, I am. That's the painting I switched."

I was sure it wouldn't be the same one. "Then I'm stumped." I brought up the frame pieces and laid them out on the table.

Maxine asked how I knew what went where. I told her about the lettering.

"Everyone take a look and tell me if you see anything someone would get killed over."

They passed the pieces around. They turned the pieces over and held them up to the light. Nothing.

"Sorry, Spencer," said Maxine.

"Me too. There's something I'm missing. But I have another thought. Maybe Gunderson never put whatever it is on the frame."

Maxine's eyes widened. "That makes sense, Spencer."

I turned to Cletis. "Cletis, did you see Gunderson working on the frame?"

"No. I asked him about it. He said he'd frame it himself. I left before he started."

On the way back, I thought about the possibilities. I wanted to get into Gunderson's house.

I didn't pass a single car on the way back. When I stopped at the door, I heard the phone ringing. I'd left the door open. It was Rosie. I asked her to hang on while I brought in the evidence.

Chapter 48

ey Spencer. I got your machine at home and thought you might be up there. You're doing a lot of driving these days."

"A lot more than I want. I'd love to stay for more than two days."

"I bet. You going to tell me what happened?"

"Didn't you hear?" I arranged pillows on the couch, sat back, and set the phone on my lap.

"You mean you got a tip and followed Vitale to that warehouse and shot him when he pulled a knife even though he was holding onto Pitcher and Steele shot another guy who was going to put a knife in your back story? That story?"

"Yeah, that's the one."

"You've gotta be kidding."

"Pardon?"

"How dumb do I look?"

"Not at all dumb."

"Then give, P.I."

"Not comfortable on the phone, Rosie. Let's have dinner tomorrow night. Come on over about six and I'll grill some steaks."

"And you'll tell me then?"

"We'll see. Why don't you ask Pitcher?"

"I did. She said a guy in a cape with a big red S on the front suddenly appeared and she doesn't remember much after that."

Good for you, Pitcher, I thought. I liked that girl.

"She was probably hallucinating after what she'd been through."

"Uh huh." I switched ears. "You find anything in Vitale's apartment?"

"Really? I guess I forgot how this works—I tell you everything we have and you tell me nothing."

"Come on, Rosie. There's a lot involved here. I'll tell you as much as I can tomorrow."

I heard a long sigh. "Okay. We'll follow up with the Door County Sheriff and Chief Iverson, but we found a Door County map and a receipt from one of the marinas up there. There was also a small scrap of paper that had *Green and Blue* written on it. But mostly we found the painting *Harbor Nights*. The frame was torn apart."

"Good thing criminals aren't that smart."

"Good thing."

"How about Bloom?"

"Disappeared. The gallery is closed, which makes me think he's in on it, too."

"I wonder how he was disappeared."

"Meaning?"

"Meaning did he disappear on his own, or did somebody else disappear him?"

"Who are we talking about?"

"Well, I think all this started with Maggio. He's perfectly capable of disappearing people. If Bloom was on Maggio's payroll he may be cleaning up loose ends. Maggio is still missing something and he isn't happy about it."

"And you think Bloom was working with Vitale?"

"Actually, I don't. I think Vitale was stealing from Bloom and Bloom was just the victim. But Bloom was obviously in on whatever was going on, and Vitale didn't know that he was really stealing from Maggio. He was dumb, but not that dumb."

"And Cletis is out of it?"

"Yeah. I think his dumb days are over. He has a job and a good woman and I think he wants to keep them."

We were quiet for a minute.

"I do have something and would like to know what you want me to do with it."

"And that would be?"

"I found *Blue and Green*."

"You did? Where?" she asked excitedly.

I told her about the letter and the cave.

"That's pretty amazing. I'd like to see that sometime."

"Sure. Come on up."

"So what's the big secret?"

I took a deep breath. "That I don't know. I've looked at every inch and found nothing."

"Maybe another set of eyes."

"I had four sets. Still nothing. But here's my question. You want me to bring it back or give it to Iverson?"

"Well, I'd love to see it. And we'd love to have the evidence."

"But?"

Silence.

"No but. Bring it back. It was taken from Simmons so it's our case. We'll share information with Iverson."

"Okay by me."

"Anything else?"

"Yeah." I told her about my Gunderson theory.

"Certainly possible. But what did he do with it, whatever *it* is?"

"Don't know. Maybe it's at his house. I'll get Paul next week and go have a look."

"Anything else?" Rosie asked.

"That's all I've got, Rosie."

"For the moment."

"Yeah, see you tomorrow."

"Adios."

I hung up the phone and put it back on the table.

I yawned and thought about what to tell Rosie. I wanted to tell her all of it but knew I couldn't. There were parts that would probably put her in a tough position. Kidnapping was a crime. Technically, it was Vitale's decision to come along, but if he was alive his lawyer would be arguing a pretty strong point. And I certainly couldn't tell Rosie about Iverson. Then I wondered how this would be different if Vitale had lived. Steele had said there were a lot of things we hadn't thought of. That was one of them. It wouldn't have gone well for us in court.

There wouldn't be many questions asked Monday morning because they had some easy answers that tied everything up in a neat package. And because we got Pitcher back, they weren't going to start untying any of the knots. I knew I could get away with that because there wasn't anyone else alive to contest our story. I had gotten lucky. But I decided it didn't matter—I had decided to do whatever it took to get Pitcher back. I was trying hard to hang onto that as my motivation for killing Vitale. I wanted to believe that the fact that I had gotten the bastard who killed Kathleen was just a bonus.

Chapter 49

Rosie arrived a little before six looking like something out of a Hayley Mills movie. She wore a summer dress done in bright colors that came to just below her knees and looked like it was blowing in the breeze when she walked. Her work ponytail was gone and her auburn hair flowed down onto her shoulders. When I opened the door, she took my breath away. I told her she looked lovely.

"Thanks, Spencer," she said with a bright smile. "But don't let the look fool you. Under the lovely is a tough broad who won't be so lovely if she doesn't get what she wants."

"Yeah, I was afraid of that. Let's have a leisurely dinner so I can buy some time."

She laughed. "Okay, but first I want to see the frame."

As I led her into the kitchen, she said, "I told Lieutenant Powolski I was coming here tonight to grill you and asked if he wanted to come. He declined. He said he didn't want to know any more than he already does. And he told me I didn't either. I asked if that was an order and he said, no, just a suggestion."

"A suggestion you're obviously ignoring," I said with a frown.

The pieces of the frame were propped up in a corner next to the counter. I brought them to the table and arranged them.

She just looked at them for a few minutes. "So this is what all the trouble is about. Three people dead over these and you have them lying against your counter." She gave me a wry smile.

I didn't respond.

She picked up a piece as I got out the rib-eyes and headed for the deck. When I got back, she was holding one of the short legs straight out in front of her.

"Anything?" I asked, without much hope.

She shook her head. "Just looks like a frame to me."

"Yeah, me too."

She put the pieces back in the corner and asked if she could help.

"You can get out the salad and toss in some dressing and cut the French bread."

Green beans were cooking on the stove.

We both liked our meat medium rare so it didn't take long.

I opened a Schlitz for me and a Harp for Rosie.

Dinner was a success. We just chatted about nothing in particular. I knew she was dying to ask questions, but was holding to the agreement. As soon as the dishes were rinsed she gave me a look that meant she wasn't going to wait any longer.

I put the last plate in the dishwasher and said, "How about dessert? I have cherry pie."

"You're done stalling."

"Okay, let's move to the couch."

We got comfortable, me on an end and Rosie in the middle with her legs tucked up under her.

"So go ahead," she said.

"Go ahead, what?"

"Tell me."

I took a deep breath and let it out slowly. I had given some thought as to how to do this. "Why don't you just ask questions. There are some things I just can't share. If I can't answer something, I'll tell you."

"Fair enough. Let's start with who your tip came from."

"Come on, Rosie. You wouldn't give up an informant. You expect me to?"

"You said to ask. If I guess would you tell me?"

"Rosie!"

She laughed. She and Maxine had laughs that were enticing.

"You didn't get a phone call. Your line was tapped. So how did you get that tip?"

"Okay, I'll tell you this much. I did get a phone call. I hope you stay up all night trying to figure it out."

She looked at me with amazement. "The tip is on tape?"

"It is."

"Well, I know what I'm doing tomorrow."

"Be my guest. Good luck."

"So you got this tip with the address on Adams and you show up when Vitale happens to be there."

I scrunched up my face and squinted.

"You didn't?"

"I didn't."

"Is that all I get?" She let one leg dangle over the edge of the couch. It was a very nice leg.

"I had no idea where he was keeping Pitcher."

Her jaw dropped.

"Are you sure you want to know?"

She nodded quickly with wide eyes.

"And it goes no farther than you?"

"Cross my heart." She did.

"Does the address 4167 N. Pulaski mean anything to you?"

"Yes. It's one of our safe houses. But how did you get that address?"

I just looked at her.

It dawned on her pretty quickly. "Steele."

"Well, check the window in the bedroom. Somebody could escape out that window."

She looked confused. "What the hell are you talking about?"

"I asked Vitale if he was involved in the painting thefts and murders and kidnapping. He denied it and told me to get lost. I told him I didn't believe him. He didn't much care. I told him I had someone who could straighten it out who had seen someone with Pitcher and convinced him to come to the apartment for a meeting. If it wasn't Vitale he was free to go."

"And he just let you take him there?"

"Well, not exactly. I introduced him to my friends Smith and Wesson and convinced him I'd use it if he didn't come along."

"And where did all this happen?"

"On the street in front of his apartment building."

She gave me a dismayed look. "Spencer, I wanted you to tell me what happened, not make up some crazy story to get rid of me."

I shrugged and raised my eyebrows.

She cocked her head in my direction. "Are you telling me you're not making this up?"

"That's what I'm telling you."

She shook her head. "Okay, continue. But if I was standing on a public street I wouldn't care if you had a gun or not. No one is going to shoot someone with witnesses all around."

"I would normally agree. But I also convinced him I didn't care about the witnesses. My friend was dead and I was going to kill him if he was the one who killed her. I didn't care who saw me do it. His only chance was to meet my witness or I'd kill him right there."

"Who was your witness?"

"I didn't have one."

She just stared at me with her mouth half open.

"I can stop anytime, Rosie."

"Oh, please, no. I'm dying to hear what's next. This is better than TV. How were you going to identify him without a witness?"

"I wasn't."

"You weren't." She looked at me like I was crazy.

"No. I wasn't. I didn't care."

"You were going to shoot him without knowing if he was guilty?"

"Rosie! I'm not a murderer."

She spread her hands palms up and turned toward me on the couch with both feet on the floor. "Crazy people do crazy things, and I think you've lost your marbles."

I ignored that statement. "I wanted *him* to tell me if he was guilty."

"And he was just going to volunteer that?"

"Well, yes. But not verbally."

Her *are you crazy* look turned into something that also included sympathy, like I had lost my mind.

"Would you like a beer or wine?"

"No, I need every bit of my wits to follow this."

"Mind if I get one?"

"Yes. Seems like you've had enough. How was he going to tell you?"

"Would you agree that if he led me to where he was keeping Pitcher, that would do it?"

"Of course. And you thought he was just going to volunteer that information?"

"No. Of course not. But if he was guilty he'd know he was in trouble as soon as my witness showed up."

"So?"

"So, if you were in his shoes, what would you do?"

"You mean if I had some crazy guy who was going to shoot me if his witness fingered me and I knew I was guilty so whoever the witness was would certainly finger me?"

"Exactly. What would you do?"

She shrugged. "I'd try and escape."

"Bingo!"

She still looked confused.

"Figure it out, Rosie. I'm doing all the work here."

"What?" She stood up with her hands on her hips. "Figure what out?"

"What happened. You have all the pieces, and I gave you a clue."

She sat back down, folded her hands in her lap, and stared at them.

Still staring at them, she asked, "The window?"

"Yes."

Looking up at me, she said, "You wanted him to escape?"

I nodded.

"So you could follow him?"

I nodded again.

She nodded slowly. "Okay, maybe you're not entirely crazy." She was quiet for a few minutes.

"I still don't understand."

"What?"

"It doesn't make sense. Do I have this right? You didn't have a witness so what you were after is where Pitcher was. And if Vitale was the guy, he'd lead you there."

"Right."

"And you let him escape so he would do just that."

"Yes."

"Still not making sense, Spencer."

"What?"

"Even if he was the kidnapper, why would he go to where he had Pitcher? Why wouldn't he just go home?"

"Because I also told him we had found Pitcher, but she couldn't identify her kidnapper. She couldn't remember anything. He'd want to go check."

"And he believed all these suppositions?"

"Why not? He thought I'd kill him."

"Okay, let's say I understand all this. He escapes out the window. How did he get the chance to do that? I'd assume you'd keep an eye on him."

"I told him I had to have a chat with my witness before he saw Vitale, so I closed the door to the bedroom, and he figured it out. By the way, probably not a good idea to have a safe house with a fire escape right outside the window."

"Thanks for the advice. I'll tell the captain. But most of our witnesses don't want to escape."

I gave her a disgusted look. "I didn't mean they'd want to get out. Someone else could get in."

She nodded. "I'll mention it. Did you see him go out the window?"

"Nope. The door was closed."

"Then how did you follow him?"

"I didn't."

"No, of course not. I feel like I'm in a *Who's On First* routine here. So what happened?"

"Figure it out." I folded my arms across my chest.

It didn't take her long to come up with Steele.

"So Steele is waiting outside. And you're counting on Steele being able to follow a guy on foot. What if Vitale grabbed a cab?"

"He did."

She shook her head. "Okay. I'll take that beer."

"Another Harp?"

"Sure. Make it two."

I laughed and got the beers. One was for me. And while I was popping off the caps I decided to stop torturing her.

I handed Rosie a Harp and took a long drink of Schlitz. It hit the spot. "The plan *depended* on him grabbing a cab."

"But how would Steele follow him? He'd be on foot until Vitale got the cab. And then Steele wouldn't have his car. And you couldn't count on another cab being there. And what if Steele lost him?"

"Lean back and get comfy."

She did.

"Like I said, him grabbing a cab was a big part of the plan. Steele said the guy went down the fire escape like a bat out of hell and ran toward the street. And there was a cab just dropping off a passenger. Vitale hopped in."

"Well that was awfully lucky."

"And Steele followed him to the address on Adams."

"Sure he did. You took a chance on him losing the cab in traffic?"

I shook my head slowly from side to side. "No, no chance involved."

"Lots of chance involved in this whole damned thing! You're just not this stupid!"

"Thanks. I appreciate that. Are you listening?"

"Sure. You ready to tell me the real story?"

I laughed. "I have been, Rosie."

She started to say something and I put my hand up.

"Vitale runs out of the alley and finds a cab just dropping off a passenger. It's his lucky day. He jumps in and gives the cabbie the address on Adams. And Steele pulls out and follows the cab."

"Back up a few minutes to the part about losing him in traffic."

I shook my head. "Not if the cabbie is a pal of Steele's."

Her jaw dropped again and she stared at me. Her mouth slowly closed and it started to dawn on her.

"You knew he would escape. And you had the cab waiting to take him to Pitcher. And the cabbie would make sure he didn't lose Steele."

"Yes."

"So there's a cabbie who knows what happened. That's not smart."

"No. That wouldn't be. But he wasn't a cabbie."

"Who was he?"

I shook my head. "Can't say."

"Okay, but whoever it is might spill the beans."

"Not going to happen."

"What makes you so sure?"

"Because of who it was."

"I'd really like to know."

"I bet you would. Sorry. I told you there were questions I wouldn't answer."

She looked disappointed. "I need a potty break. Be right back."

I watched her drift out of the room, laid my head back, and closed my eyes.

***

When she came back in, she asked me to stand up. She put her arms around me and gave me a hug.

"That's amazing, Spencer. And brilliant. Must be nice not to have to follow the laws." But there was a sparkle in her eyes.

I gave her my best hurt look.

She squeezed me and said, "I'm sort of teasing, and I'm sort of jealous. You do things I can't. You really went out on a limb. What if it wasn't Vitale?"

"It was."

"Yes, but you weren't sure of that. If it wasn't, your deadline comes and goes and so does Pitcher."

"I was pretty sure."

"Big chance to take on just one of your gut feelings."

"Remember, I had a tip. And that's *all* I had."

"A tip that didn't give you an address."

"No. But a tip that pointed me toward Vitale."

"And you were sure enough to set all that up?"

"I was."

"And you're not going to tell me who."

I took a deep breath, let it out slowly, and took a drink. "If I tell you, you can't say who—ever."

She nodded.

"Maggio."

She jumped up again and looked down at me. "Maggio? Maggio! All this is based on *his* word?"

"Yup."

"That's amazing. You did all that based on the word of the head of organized crime in Chicago?"

"I did."

She just looked at me with her mouth half open. "Why?"

"Because I knew the tip was good. He really doesn't like to lose. He found out Vitale was trying to steal from him and he wanted to get even."

"So why involve you? This guy is good at getting even. We've got a score of deaths we can't pin on him, but we know it's him, or his goons."

"Because, if *I* get Vitale, Maggio's not a suspect. And Maggio knew I wanted to get Vitale. He knows what it feels like to want revenge. He gave me that chance."

"Jesus, Spencer. You made a deal with the devil."

"I guess you could look at it like that."

"And how do you look at it?"

"He used me. But I also used him. And the result was we got Pitcher back—alive."

She looked at me with dismay. "I can't argue with that. But this is all so…"

"Done. It's done, Rosie. Let it go."

She put her arms around me again and held on tight. I held her back.

When she pulled away, she said, "Well, not quite done."

I looked at her.

"Three dead…"

"Well, technically, four. There's the other guy in the basement."

"Okay. Four and maybe five. We may never know about Bloom. And we have no idea what it was all about."

"Maybe not. Maggio knows, but I'm guessing he's not gonna talk. How about that pie?"

"Sure." She took my arm and we moved to the kitchen.

Chapter 50

I cut the pie and set a piece in front of Rosie. "Nothing better than Aunt Rose's cherry pie. Do you want ice cream?"

"No thanks. This is great."

We ate quietly for a few bites before she asked another question.

"Do I get to know what happened in the basement?"

I shook my head. "People died, Rosie. They were the bad guys, but shots were still fired, and that's more serious than what happened up till then."

"Did you shoot Vitale?"

"I did. And that's your last question. Now it's my turn."

She just stared at me.

"I'm wondering about Steele."

She looked confused. "What about him?"

"I've never been much of a Steele fan. Good cop, I guess, but not very friendly—even arrogant. But after all this, I really like the guy. He was a big part of getting Pitcher back. And even you said he's growing on you."

She ate her pie. "Yup. So what are you wondering?"

I shrugged. "I'm not sure. There's a wall there somewhere. He's not unfriendly, but not friendly either."

Rosie finished the last bite and said, "We all have our walls, Spencer. Some are taller than others."

"How tall is Steele's?"

"Pretty tall. There's something some of us know about but don't mention."

"Something you can share?"

"I suppose. But remember the 'don't mention' part."

"Sure."

She put down her fork and continued. "He came here from New York after his wife committed suicide—drug overdose."

"Jesus, Rosie. That's awful. Do you know why?"

She nodded. "Their son disappeared. He was twelve. Never found him. Steele took some time off and then came to Chicago. But tough to just walk away from all that."

"I guess. The poor guy." I cut off a bite of pie and thought about how the past can stay with a person. I was considering sharing something with Rosie when she spoke.

"You said I couldn't ask any more questions. Can I make a statement?"

"Sure."

"I think there was somebody in the basement besides you and Steele."

"There was. There was Pitcher and Vitale and whoever the other dead guy was."

She shook her head while taking another bite. "I mean another somebody on *your* side."

"And why would you think that?"

"It works better that way."

"Well, think whatever you like. I'm done talking."

"Okay. You'd better just hope whoever it is never talks."

"I'm not worried. All that matters to me is that Pitcher is safe. Everything we did was worth it. She is one mighty brave woman."

"She is." She looked at me with a squint. "Are you interested?"

"In Pitcher?" I laughed. "No. She's not my type."

"And not very experienced when it comes to men. She told me she has never had a date with just one guy."

"That's hard to believe."

"Yup. Said she always went out in groups. You were probably the first guy she ever sat across from in a booth alone."

I ate the last of my pie. "You know, maybe a little makeup and some hair styling and she wouldn't be so homely looking."

"Spencer! I'm surprised at you. I never thought I'd hear that coming out of *your* mouth."

"I just meant…"

"I know what you meant. You know, it's not what's on the outside, it's what's on the inside that counts."

"I know, I was just…" And I stopped dead with a look on my face that got Rosie's attention.

"What, Spencer?"

"It's what's on the inside."

"Yeah, she's a wonderful person. Some guy…"

"I'm not talking about Pitcher." I got up and got the frame pieces. "This frame is about an inch thick."

"So?"

"So, there's been something bothering me ever since I found Gunderson's body."

"What?"

"There were a lot of tools in his shop, including a drill."

"So?"

"So, would a framer have a drill?"

She shrugged.

"What if he drilled a hole in the frame and whatever we're looking for is *inside* the frame?"

"Possible, but we've looked all over the frame. I didn't see any holes."

"Neither did I, but maybe we need to look closer."

"Hard to miss a hole, Spencer."

"Yeah, you would think so. But what if he drilled it, put something in the hole, and then plugged it and covered it."

"We'd still see it."

"If I did it, yes. But Cletis said Gunderson was a genius with wood. There were beautiful duck decoys in his shop. I bet he could cover up a hole so you wouldn't notice."

"All right. Let's go with that. What next?"

"X-ray the frame."

She laughed. "Sure. We'll stop at the hospital and ask if they'll x-ray some wood."

"Well, why not?"

"Okay, I'll check in the morning." She picked up a piece and looked closely.

I left the kitchen and came back a minute later with two magnifying glasses. I handed one to Rosie. "Start looking."

She did. I picked up a piece and joined her. After five minutes she called my name.

"Look where my finger is."

I did. There was a partial arc, about the size of the bit that was in the drill, that was a slightly different color from the rest of the frame. I got a work light, set it up on the table, and held the frame under the light. That helped a little. It looked different from the rest of the frame.

"Nice catch, Rosie."

"What next?"

"I'll be right back."

I returned with Dad's tool box, got out a small chisel, and started digging at the spot. It didn't take much to expose part of a hole. I dug some more and found the top of a tiny cylinder. When I turned the frame over and tapped on the other side, the cylinder barely came out of the hole. More tapping didn't help. Rosie handed me a pair of pliers and I barely grabbed the end of the cylinder. I pulled carefully and it came out.

It was a plastic tube about an inch long. I pulled off the cap and dumped it out on the table.

Rosie and I looked at each other.

"Are those diamonds?" she asked.

"Look like diamonds to me."

"Maybe they're fake."

"Maybe, but Maggio isn't going to go through all this for fake diamonds."

"Wow. Look at those."

There were eight diamonds, all sparkling in the light.

"How much do you think they're worth, Spencer?"

"Enough to kill people for."

"I wonder if there are more."

"Probably, but I'm done digging. Let the lab take it from here."

She sat down. "So Gunderson was in on this?"

"I'd bet my house on it. He told Cletis he'd frame *Green and Blue* personally. He wanted to hide the diamonds. He was the link between the buyer and the seller."

"Where do you think they came from?"

"No idea. We'll probably never know, but my guess is they came by boat, maybe from up north. Easy to move something like this by water, maybe even from Canada. But almost everyone who might know for sure is dead."

"Except Maggio."

"Except Maggio. And I'm not going to ask him."

"This'll hit the news. He won't be happy. Remember, he doesn't like to lose."

I shut off the light. "No, he doesn't. But losing to a competitor or an employee trying to steal from him is one thing. Losing to the police is an occupational hazard—it's just business."

"I sure hope so for your sake." She brushed the wood shavings into her hand and threw them in the garbage.

"So what do we do with this?" I asked.

"I say we take it to the station tonight—unless you want to be responsible for the diamonds?"

"I think not. How about you run them in on your way home. I'm going to call Stosh and tell him about this."

"How about you follow me over there. I'm not going alone."

"Okay." I grabbed my gun.

A half hour later I backed out of the drive and followed Rosie to the station where two detectives were waiting for us. While Rosie was filling out the paperwork, Stosh walked in.

"Nice job, you two."

"Thanks, Lieutenant," I responded. "All in a night's work."

"Remember you have an interview in the morning?"

"Yup. You see any problems?"

"No. I've talked with the captain of the third. They just need to wrap it up. Just stick to that story and nobody will ask any questions. No one wants this to be complicated."

"Not a problem."

We shook hands.

"And after the interview why don't you take some time off. You've earned a vacation." He turned to Rosie. "You have any time coming, Lonnigan?"

"I do."

"Well, take it." He turned and looked at me with raised eyebrows.

I just looked back.

He rolled his eyes and walked out.

I said goodbye to Rosie and followed Stosh out to the parking lot, catching up to him as he was getting into his car.

He looked disgusted. "How much hint do you need, Spencer?"

"I got the hint. But I need some time by myself."

"Yeah, seems like you've had a lot of that. Time you had some time *not* by yourself. And I can't think of anyone better not to be by yourself with than Rosie."

"Thanks for thinking of me. I'll think about it."

"You do that. And Spencer, if you decide to be alone, you need to tell her why. Good night, kid."

"Good night, Stosh."

I stood and watched him pull away. And on the way home I thought about being alone. I had two wonderful women who I enjoyed being with, and I was pretty sure either one would love to spend some time at the cottage. But for the moment, I needed to get over the girl I didn't have that option with anymore.

Chapter 51

The interview went just as easily as Stosh said it would. I kept waiting for them to ask me more questions, but they kept asking the same ones over and over. I had the feeling they were just taking up time. They did say they needed to be sure of the story.

I called Stosh when I got home and told him about the interview. He told me the lab had found no prints on the clown photo but had found three more vials of diamonds in the frame. Maggio's diamond pipeline was closed—at least this one.

I packed enough clothes for a week and headed north—again. On the way I had plenty of time to think about the last ten days. I did get lucky, but as Dad said, lucky people make their own luck. I had nothing to lose with the Vitale plan. It was the only option I had, and it was worth breaking some rules to try it.

The only loose end was Bloom and we'd probably never find him. I figured Maggio took care of him. But if that happened, Bloom didn't deserve it—he wasn't the one cheating Maggio. But if you decide to do business with Maggio, you never know what the consequences might be. He doesn't ask too many questions.

As I drove, I started to work on a new plan. I don't know how it started, but I all of a sudden realized there was a frame shop for sale—probably pretty cheap. Something dependable to fall back on might be a good idea. The P.I. business wasn't all that steady. I didn't have to worry about money but something else to do might be fun. The more I drove, the more excited I got.

I got a drive-through burger and fries and ate while I was driving.

A little after four, I pulled into the inn parking lot. The only greeter on the porch was Amelie and she wasn't very excited to see me.

The lobby was empty, but I could smell pies baking. I found Aunt Rose in the kitchen just pulling two pies out of the oven.

"Is one of those for me?"

She put the pies on cooling racks on the counter and gave me a hug. "*Now* are you staying for a while?"

"That's my plan. I packed for a week, but I could do some wash and stay longer."

"Good. Let's spend some porch time."

"Just what the doctor ordered, Aunt Rose." Aunt Rose mentioned "porch time" to all of her guests. And it was mentioned in the brochures. Slow down and enjoy watching the world go by. Sit on the porch and read a book, chat with guests, or take a nap. Not easy for most people to do, but those who did always came back to do it again.

I asked Aunt Rose where Peggy Sue and Cletis were.

"Last I saw, they were out back in the gazebo."

I kissed her on the cheek. "Thanks. I'll be back for pie."

The limestone path around the inn wound through the garden back to the gazebo. I stopped in the garden where I could see them holding hands and looking pretty happy. I was glad Cletis didn't lose her.

"Hi. Looks like you're enjoying the afternoon," I said.

"Thanks to you," said Peggy Sue with a smile.

"Well, I just gave you the opportunity. Up to you to make something of it. How's the new job, Cletis?"

"Going okay, Mr. Manning. Nice people there."

"And Peggy Sue? How do you like it here?"

"I love it," she said with a smile. Then she looked sad and looked down. "But your aunt doesn't really need me. She and Maxine handle things pretty well. We talked about it and she said she could probably use me part-time, but there just isn't enough work for a real job."

I sat down next to Peggy Sue. "Yeah, I figured it wouldn't be permanent."

"She said I could keep working till we find a place. But I know she's just being nice. I'd rather pull my own weight."

"Good for you, Peggy Sue. That's something every employer looks for, but it's pretty rare these days. Have you looked around?"

She looked discouraged. "Yes. But so far, nothing. All the summer jobs are filled, and it will only get worse after the tourist season."

"That's true." I rubbed my chin and squinted at her. "Maybe you can help me out."

"How could I help *you* out?"

"Well, I've wanted to try my hand at business, and I hear there's a frame store that'll probably be for sale."

"So how can I help?"

"I'm going to need someone to run the place. Would you be interested?"

Her eyes widened and she smiled from ear to ear. "Would I!" Then she calmed down. "But you'd run it, wouldn't you?"

"Heck no. I don't want to work—I just want to own it and stop in for coffee once in a while."

"And you want me?"

"I can't think of anyone better."

She smiled again.

I rubbed my chin again and looked out into the yard. "But there's a problem."

"I knew there would be," she said quietly.

"Yup, there sure is. I don't know anything about frames. I'd need someone to handle the shop." I looked back at her. "You know anybody who knows anything about frames?"

She perked up. "How about Cletis? He already... Hey, you're kidding me aren't you?"

I smiled, too. "Yes, I'm sorry. Cletis, you interested?"

His face lit up. "Sure am Mr. Manning! I can do everything Mr. Gunderson did. Well, except the ducks."

I nodded. "Don't need the ducks, Cletis. You two think you could work together?"

They both nodded. Cletis looked over at Peggy Sue. "We could do anything together."

"Great. I have no idea how long this will take, but I'll get the ball rolling. I'm sure Aunt Rose will wait."

With a tear in her eye, Peggy Sue kissed me on the cheek. "Thanks, Spencer. I can't tell you how much this means to us." She looked over at Cletis and smiled.

"Hey, you're the ones doing me a favor. Hard to get good help these days."

I stood up. "Can I interest you in some cherry pie?"

We all headed for the kitchen and some of Aunt Rose's magic.

If you liked this book, please post a review at:
Amazon.com/dp/193954811X

To be notified of other Rick Polad books, go to
rickpolad.com and click "Join Us"

"Like" Spencer at Facebook.com/SpencerManningMysteries

Made in the USA
Lexington, KY
29 August 2014